"My buggy is just around the corner. Would you care to share a ride?" Roman asked.

There wasn't a cloud in the sky. He had no reason to offer her a lift today. "It doesn't look like rain."

"I thought since we were going the same way…" His voice trailed off. He cocked an eyebrow and waited.

It was a long walk after a long day, but she'd rather crawl home on her hands and knees than spend another minute in his company. Thankfully, Joann managed not to blurt out her opinion. "I have errands to run. I'll see you tomorrow."

Tomorrow would arrive all too quickly.

"Suit yourself." Without another word, he walked away and turned the corner.

Had he actually sounded disappointed?

Books by Patricia Davids

Love Inspired

His Bundle of Love
Love Thine Enemy
Prodigal Daughter
The Color of Courage
Military Daddy
A Matter of the Heart
A Military Match
A Family for Thanksgiving
*Katie's Redemption
*The Doctor's Blessing
*An Amish Christmas
*The Farmer Next Door
*The Christmas Quilt
*A Home for Hannah
*A Hope Springs Christmas
*Plain Admirer

*Brides of Amish Country

Love Inspired Suspense

A Cloud of Suspicion
Speed Trap

PATRICIA DAVIDS

After thirty-five years as a nurse, Pat has hung up her stethoscope to become a full-time writer. She enjoys spending her new free time visiting her grandchildren, doing some long-overdue yard work and traveling to research her story locations. She resides in Wichita, Kansas. Pat always enjoys hearing from her readers. You can visit her on the web at www.patriciadavids.com.

Plain Admirer

Patricia Davids

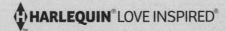

Recycling programs
for this product may
not exist in your area.

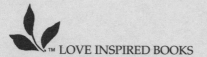 ™ LOVE INSPIRED BOOKS

ISBN-13: 978-0-373-87817-8

PLAIN ADMIRER

www.LoveInspiredBooks.com

Printed in U.S.A.

And God blessed them, and God said unto them,
Be fruitful, and multiply, and replenish the earth,
and subdue it: and have dominion over the fish
of the sea, and over the fowl of the air, and over
every living thing that moveth upon the earth.
—*Genesis* 1:28

This book is lovingly dedicated to my father, Clarence—a man who can look at any stretch of water and tell just where the fish are. Thanks for teaching me, my daughter and my grandchildren to bait our own hooks. Love you. Let's go fishing soon.

Chapter One

"This isn't easy to say, but I have to let you go, Joann. I'm sure you understand."

"You're firing me?" Joann Yoder faced her boss across the cluttered desk in his office. For once, she wasn't tempted to straighten up for him. And she didn't understand.

"*Ja.* I'm sorry."

Otis Miller didn't look the least bit sorry. Certainly not as sorry as she was to be losing a job she really needed. A job she loved. Why was this happening? Why now, when she was so close to realizing her dream?

She'd only been at Miller Press for five months, but working as an assistant editor and office manager at the Amish-owned publishing house was everything she'd ever wanted. How could it end so quickly? If she knew what she had done wrong, she could fix it. "At least tell me why."

He sighed heavily, as if disappointed she hadn't accepted her dismissal without question. "You knew when you came over from the bookstore that this might not be a permanent position."

Joann had moved from a part-time job at the bookstore next door to help at the printing shop after Otis's elder brother suffered a heart attack. When he passed away a few weeks later, Joann had assumed she would be able to keep his job. She loved gathering articles for their monthly magazine and weekly newspaper, as well as making sure the office ran smoothly and customers received the best possible attention. She dropped her gaze to her hands clenched tightly in her lap and struggled to hang on to her dignity. Tears pricked the back of her eyelids, but she refused to cry. "You told me I was doing a good job."

"You have been. Better than I expected, but I'm giving Roman Weaver your position. I don't need to tell you why."

"*Nee,* you don't." Like everyone in the Amish community of Hope Springs, Ohio, she was aware of the trouble that had visited the Weaver family. She hated that her compassion struggled so mightily with her desire to support herself. This job was proof that her intelligence mattered. She might be the "bookworm" her brothers had often called her, but here she had a chance to put her learning to good use. Now it was all being taken away.

She couldn't let it go without a fight. She looked up and blurted, "Does he really need the job more than I do?"

Otis didn't like conflict. He leaned back in his chair and folded his arms across his broad chest. "Roman has large medical bills to pay."

"But the church held an auction to help raise money for him."

"He and his family are grateful for all the help they received, but they are still struggling."

She'd lost, and she knew it. Only a hint of the bitterness she felt slipped through in her words. "Plus, he's your nephew."

"That, too," Otis admitted without any sign of embarrassment. Family came only after God in their Amish way of life.

Roman Weaver had had it rough, there was no denying that. It was a blessing that he hadn't lost his arm after a pickup truck smashed into his buggy. Unfortunately, his damaged left arm was now paralyzed and useless. She'd seen him at the church meetings wearing a heavy sling and heard her brothers say the physical therapy he needed was expensive and draining his family's resources.

Her heart went out to him and his family, but why should she be the one to lose her job? There were others who worked for Miller Press.

She didn't bother to voice that thought. She already knew why she had been chosen. Because she was a woman.

Joann had no illusions about the male-dominated society she lived in. Unmarried Amish women could hold a job, but they gave it up when they married to make a home for their husband and children. A married woman could work outside the home, but only if her husband agreed to it.

Amish marriage was a partnership where each man and woman knew and respected their roles within the *Ordnung,* the laws of their Amish church. Men were the head of the household. Joann didn't disagree with any of it. At least, not very much.

It was just that she had no desire to spend the rest of her life living with her brothers, moving from one house to another and being an unwanted burden to their families. She'd never had a come-calling boyfriend, although she'd accepted a ride home from the singings with a few fellas in her youth. She'd never received an offer of marriage. And at the advanced age of twenty-six, it wasn't likely she would.

Besides, there wasn't anyone in Hope Springs she would consider spending the rest of her life with. As the years had gone by, she'd begun to accept that she would always be a maiden aunt. Maybe she'd get a cat one day.

Otis folded his hands together on his desk. "I am sorry, Joann. Roman needs the job. He can't work in the sawmill with only one good arm. It's too dangerous."

"I must work, too. My brothers have many children. I don't wish to burden them by having them take care of me, as well."

"Come now, you're being unreasonable. Your brothers do not begrudge you room and board."

"They would never say it, but I think they do." She knew her three brothers had taken her in out of a strong sense of duty after their parents died and not because of brotherly love. Hadn't they decided her living arrangements among themselves without consulting her? She stayed with each brother for four months. At the end of that time, she moved to the next brother's home. By the end of the year, she was back where she had started. She always had a roof over her head, but she didn't have a home.

She wanted a home of her own, but that wasn't going to happen without a good-paying job.

"Joann, think of Roman. Where is your Christian compassion?"

"I left it at home in a jar."

Otis scowled at her flippancy. She blushed at her own audacity. Modesty and humility were the aspirations of every Amish woman, but sometimes things slipped out of her mouth before she had time to think.

Why couldn't someone else give Roman a job he could manage? She dreamed of having a home of her own, a small house at the edge of the woods where she could keep her books and compile her nature notes and observations unhindered by her nieces and nephews. Best of all, she'd be able to go fishing whenever she wanted without her family's sarcastic comments about wasting her time. The only way she could accomplish that was by earning her own money.

She was so close to realizing her dream. The very house she wanted was coming up for sale. The owners, her friends Sarah and Levi Beachy, were willing to sell to her and finance her if she could come up with the down payment by the end of September. If she couldn't raise the agreed-upon amount, they would have to sell to another Amish family. They needed the money to make improvements to their business before winter.

What only a week ago had seemed like a sure thing, a gift from God, was now slipping out of her grasp. Joann didn't want to beg, but she would. "Can't you do anything for me, Otis? You know I'm a hard worker."

"All I can offer you is a part-time position—"

"I'll take it."

"One day a week on the cleaning staff."

"Oh." Her last bit of hope vanished. Her book learning wouldn't be needed while she swept the floors and emptied wastepaper baskets.

Otis leaned back in his chair. "Of course, your part-time position at the bookstore is yours if you want it."

A part-time salary would be far less than she needed. Still, it was better than nothing. She wasn't proud. She'd do a good job for him. In time, she might even get a chance at an editorial position again. Only God knew what the future held.

She nodded once. "I would be grateful for such work."

Otis rose to his feet. "*Goot.* You'll work afternoons Monday through Wednesday at the bookstore, and here on Saturdays. But there is something I need you to do for me before you switch jobs."

"What is that?"

"I need you to show Roman how we do things here. He's only worked in the sawmill and on the farm. The publishing business is foreign to him. I'm sure it won't take you more than two weeks to show him the ropes. He's a bright fellow. He'll catch on quickly. You can do that, can't you?"

He gets my job, but I have to show him how to do it? Where is the justice in that? She kept her face carefully blank.

Otis scowled again. "Well?"

"I'll be glad to show Roman all I've learned." It wasn't a complete lie, but it was close. She would do it, but she wouldn't be happy about it.

Otis nodded and came around the desk. "Fine. I hope my nephew can start on Monday morning. After you get him up to speed, you can return to the bookstore. That's all, you can go home now."

"Danki." She rose from her seat and headed for the door. Pulling it open, she saw the man who was taking her job sitting quietly in a chair across the room. Did he know or care that she was being cast aside for him? They had attended the same school, but he had been a year behind her.

After their school years, she saw him and his family at Sunday services, but their paths rarely crossed. He'd run with the fast crowd during their *rumspringa,* their running-around teenage years. She had chosen baptism at the age of nineteen while he hadn't joined the faith until two years ago. His circle of friends didn't include her or her family. She studied him covertly as she would one of her woodland creatures.

Roman Weaver was a good-looking fellow with a head of curly blond hair that bore the imprint of the hat he normally wore. His cheeks were lean, his chin chiseled and firm. He was clean-shaven, denoting his single status. His years of hard physical work showed in the muscular width of his shoulders crisscrossed by his suspenders. He wore a black sling on his left arm. It stood out in stark contrast to his short-sleeved white shirt. His straw hat rested on the chair arm beside him.

Compassion touched her heart when she noticed the fine lines that bracketed his mouth. Was he in pain?

He looked up as she came out of the office. His piercing blue eyes, rimmed with thick lashes, brightened. He smiled. An unfamiliar thrill fluttered in the pit of her stomach. No one had ever smiled at her with such warmth.

His dazzling gaze slid past her to settle on Otis, and Joann realized she'd been a fool to think Roman Weaver was smiling at her. She doubted he even saw her.

"Hello, *Onkel,*" Roman said, rising from his chair.

"It's *goot* to see you, nephew." Otis stepped back to give him room to enter his office. Roman walked past her without a glance.

She kept her eyes downcast as an odd stab of disappointment hit her. Why should it matter that his smile hadn't been for her? She was used to being invisible. She'd long ago given up the hope that she'd become attractive and witty. She wasn't ugly, but she had no illusions about her plain looks. She was as God had made her.

She consoled herself with the knowledge that what the Lord had held back in looks He'd more than made up for in intelligence. She was smarter than her brothers and her few friends. It wasn't anything special that she had done. She was smart the way some people were tall, because that was the way God fashioned them.

For a long time, she thought of her intellect as a burden. Then, an elderly teacher told her she was smarter than anyone he'd ever met and that God must surely have something special in mind for her. That single statement had enabled Joann to see herself in a completely new light.

Being smart wasn't a bad thing, even if some others thought it was. When she landed this job, she knew being smart was indeed a blessing.

As Roman Weaver closed the door behind him, old feelings of being left out, of being overlooked and unvalued wormed their way into her heart. They left a painful bruise she couldn't dismiss.

Crossing to her desk, she lifted her green-and-white quilted bag from the back of her chair and settled the strap on her shoulder. Roman Weaver might look past her today, but come Monday morning, he was going to find he needed her. He wouldn't look through her then.

Roman forced a bright smile to his lips in order to hide his nervousness. The summons from his uncle had come out of the blue. He had no idea what his mother's brother wanted with him, but the look on her face when she relayed the message had Roman worried. What was going on? What was wrong?

The better question might have been: What was

right? He had the answer to that one: not much in his life at the moment. The gnawing pain he endured from his injury was constant proof of that.

Otis indicated a chair. "Have a seat."

Roman did so, holding his injured arm against his chest, more from habit than a need to protect it. "I've often wondered what it is that you do here."

He glanced around the room filled with filing cabinets, books and stacks of papers. The smell of solvents and ink gave the air a harsh, sharp quality that stung his nostrils. Roman preferred the clean scent of fresh-cut wood.

His uncle was the owner of a small publishing business whose target audience was Old Order Plain People, Amish, Mennonites and Hutterites. A small bookstore next door housed a number of books he published as well as a small library. Although Roman occasionally read the magazine his uncle put out each month, he'd only visited the office and bookstore a few times. He wasn't a reader.

"How's the arm?" Otis asked.

"It's getting better." Much too slowly for Roman's liking.

"Are you in pain?"

"Some." He didn't elaborate. It was his burden to bear.

"I'm sure you're wondering why I've asked you here. Your parents came to see me last Sunday," Otis said, looking vaguely uncomfortable.

"Did they?" This was the first Roman had heard of it.

"Your father asked me for a business loan. Of course, I was happy to help. I know things have been difficult for all of you."

Roman's medical bills had already cost his family

nearly all their savings. His inability to do his job in the sawmill was cutting their productivity, making his father and his brother work even harder. If his father had come to Otis for a loan, things must be dire.

"You have my gratitude and my thanks. We will repay you as soon as we can."

"I know. I'm not worried about that. Before they left, your mother spoke privately with me. My sister is very dear to me, but I will admit to being surprised when she asked if I would offer you a job here at my office."

The muscles in Roman's jaw clenched. "I work at my father's side in the sawmill. I don't need a job. I have one," he said.

Sympathy flashed in his uncle's eyes. "You have one that you can't continue."

"My arm is better. I'm making progress." He concentrated on his fingers protruding from the sling. He was able to move his index and middle finger ever so slightly.

He could tell from the look on his uncle's face that he wasn't impressed. If only he knew how much effort it took to move any part of his hand.

"I give thanks to God for His mercy and pray for your recovery daily," Otis said. "As do your parents, but your father needs a man with two strong arms to work in the mill if he is to earn a profit and meet his obligations."

"He hasn't said this to me."

"I don't imagine he would. I'm asking you to consider what is best for your family. I have work, worthy work, for you to do that requires a good mind but not two strong arms. Besides, your mother will rest easier knowing you aren't trying to do too much."

A sick sensation settled in Roman's stomach. "She told you about the incident last week?"

"Ja."

"It was a freak accident. My sling got snagged on a log going into the saw. The strap broke and freed me." He tried to make it sound less dire than it had been. He would relive the memory of those horrible, helpless moments in his nightmares for a long time. His confidence in his ability to do the job he'd always considered his birthright had suffered a harsh blow.

"I understand you were jerked off your feet and dragged toward the saw," Otis said.

"I was never in danger of being pulled into the blade." He was sure he could have freed himself.

Maybe.

"That's not how your mother saw it."

No, it wasn't. Roman's humiliation had been made all the worse by his mother's fright. She had come into the mill to deliver his lunch and witnessed the entire thing. Her screams had alerted his father and younger brother, but no one had been close enough to help. God had answered her frantic plea and freed him in time.

"I'm sorry *Mamm* was frightened, but sawmill work is all I know. I don't see how I can be of use to you in this business," Roman said.

"I fully expect you to give me a fair day's work for your wage. Joann Yoder will teach you all you need to know about being a manager and an editor."

Roman barely heard his uncle's words. He stared at his useless arm resting in the sling. It was dead weight around his neck. He didn't want to be dead weight around his family's neck. Could he accept the humiliation of being unable to do a man's job? He wasn't sure.

All his life he'd been certain of his future. Now, he had no idea what God wanted from him.

"Say you will at least think about it, nephew. Who knows, you may find the work suits you. It would please me to think my sister's son might carry on the business my brother and I built after I'm gone."

Roman glanced at his uncle's hopeful face. He and his wife were childless, and his recently deceased older brother had never married, but Roman had no intention of giving up his eventual ownership of the sawmill. If he did accept his uncle's offer, it would only be a temporary job. "Who did you say would train me?"

"The woman you saw leaving just as you came in."

"I'm sorry, I wasn't paying attention. Is she someone I know?"

"Joann Yoder. The sister of Hebron, Ezekiel and William Yoder. I'm sure you know her."

Roman's eyebrows shot up. "The bookworm?"

Otis laughed. "I had no idea that was her nickname, but it fits."

"It was something we used to call her when we were kids in school." She was a plain, shy woman who always stayed in the background.

"Joann can teach you what you need to know about this work."

Roman clamped his lips shut and stared down at his paralyzed arm. He had trouble dressing himself. He couldn't tie his own shoes without help. He couldn't do a man's job, a job that he'd done since he was ten years old. Now, he was going to have a woman telling him how to do this job, if he took it. How much more humiliation would God ask him to bear?

He looked at his uncle. "Why can't you show me how the business is run?"

"I'll be around to answer your questions, but Joann knows the day-to-day running of the business almost as well as I do."

So, he would be stuck with Joann Yoder as a mentor if he accepted. Was she still the quiet, studious loner who chose books over games and sports?

Otis hooked his thumbs under his suspenders and rocked back on his heels. "What do you say, Roman? Will you come work for me?"

Chapter Two

Joann trudged along the quiet, tree-lined streets of Hope Springs with her head down and her carefully laid plans in shambles. Early May sunshine streamed through the branches overhead, making lace patterns on the sidewalk that danced as the wind stirred the leaves. The smell of freshly mowed grass and lilacs scented the late afternoon air.

At any other time, she would have delighted in the glorious weather, the cool breeze and the fragrant flowers blooming in profusion beside the neatly tended houses of the village. At the moment, all she could see was more years of shuffling from one house to another stretching in front of her.

If only I hadn't dared dream that I could change my life.

A small brown-and-white dog raced past her, yipping furiously. His quarry, a yellow tabby, had crossed the street just ahead of him. The cat shot up the nearest tree. From the safety of a thick branch, it growled at the dog barking and leaping below. The mutt circled the tree several times and then sat down to keep an eye on his intended victim.

As Joann came up beside the terrier mix, he looked her way. She stopped to pat his head. "I know just how you feel. So close and yet so far. Take my word for it, you wouldn't have liked the outcome if you had caught him." The cat was almost as big as the dog.

Joann walked on, wondering if there was a similar reason why she couldn't obtain the prize she had been working so hard to secure. Would the outcome have been worse than what she had now? Only the Lord knew. She had to trust in His will, but it was hard to see the good through her disappointment.

After a few more minutes, she reached the buggy shop of Levi Beachy at the edge of town. She passed it every day on her way to and from work. Across the street from the shop stood the house that had almost been hers.

Sarah Wyse, a young Amish widow, had lived there until shortly after Christmas when she married Levi. For a time they had rented the house to a young Amish couple, but they had moved away a month ago and the small, two-story house was vacant again.

Vacant and waiting for someone to move in who would love and cherish it.

Joann stopped with her hands on the gate. The picket fence needed a coat of paint. She itched to take a paintbrush to it. The lawn was well-kept, but if the home belonged to her, she would plant a row of pansies below the front porch railing and add a birdhouse in the corner of the yard. She loved to watch birds. They always seemed so happy.

She would be happy, too, if all it took to build a snug home for herself was bits of straw and twigs. However, it took more. Much more.

She gazed at the windows of the upper story. She'd

been a guest in Sarah's home several times. She knew the upstairs held two bedrooms. One for her and one for visitors. Downstairs there was a cozy sitting room with a wide brick fireplace. Off the kitchen was a room just the right size to set up a quilt frame. Joann longed for a quilt frame of her own, but she didn't have a place to keep one.

"Joann, how nice to see you," Sarah Beachy said as she came out of the shop with her arms full of upholstery material. She did all the sewing for the business, covering the buggy seats and door panels her husband made in whatever fabric the customer ordered.

"Hello, Sarah," Joann returned the greeting but couldn't manage a cheerful face for her friend.

"Joann, what's wrong?" Sarah laid her bundle on a bench outside the door and quickly crossed the narrow roadway.

Unexpected tears blurred Joann's vision. She didn't cry. She never cried. She rubbed the moisture away with her hands and folded her arms across her chest. "Nothing," she said, gazing at the ground.

"Something is definitely wrong. You're scaring me." Sarah cupped Joann's chin, lifting gently until Joann had no choice but to meet her gaze.

She swallowed and said, "I've come to tell you that you don't have to wait until September to put your house on the market. You can do it right away."

"You mean you've decided that you don't want it?"

"I'm afraid I can't afford it now."

"I don't understand. Just two weeks ago you told us you were sure you could earn the amount we agreed upon by that time."

"I was fired today."

"Fired? Why on earth would Otis Miller do that?"

"To give the job to someone who needs it more. He's keeping me on as a part-time cleaning woman, and I can have my old job at the bookstore back, but I won't earn nearly enough to pay you what you need by the end of the summer. It was really nice of you and Levi to offer to let me make payments over time, but I know how much you want to make improvements to the business before winter."

"Levi would like to get the holes in the roof fixed and a new generator for the lathe, but I would rather see you happy. If you want, I can talk to him about giving you more time. Perhaps, instead of selling it we could rent it to you. We would both be delighted to have you as our neighbor."

"*Danki,* but that isn't fair to you. Selling your house outright makes much more sense. Besides, with only a part-time job, I wouldn't be able to afford the rent, either. There will be another house for me when the time is right."

She said as much, but she wasn't sure she believed it. Her brothers didn't feel she should live alone and they weren't willing to cover the cost of another house. The local bank had already turned her down for a home loan. She didn't have enough money saved to make a substantial down payment and her employment record wasn't long enough. Only Levi and Sarah had been willing to take a chance on her.

Another home might come along in the distant future, but would it have such a sunny kitchen? Or such an ample back porch with a well-tended garden that backed up to the woods, and a fine sturdy barn for a horse and buggy? This house was perfect. It wasn't too large or too small, and it was close to work.

To the job she didn't have anymore. Her shoulders slumped.

"Come in and have a cup of tea," Sarah said. "There must be something we can do. Perhaps you can find a different job."

The wind kicked up and blew the ribbons of Joann's white prayer *kapp* across her face. She glanced toward the west. "*Danki,* but I should get going. It looks like rain is coming this way."

"I'll have one of the boys hitch up the cart and drive you."

Joann managed to smile at that. "I'm not about to get in a cart with Atlee or Moses. People still talk about how they rigged the seats to tip over backward in Daniel Hershberger's buggy and sent him and his new wife down the street, bottoms up."

Sarah tried not to laugh but lost the struggle. She giggled and pressed her hand to her lips. "It was funny, but my poor Levi was so upset. You will be safe with either one of the twins. Levi's mischief-making brothers have been a changed pair since our wedding."

"How did you manage that?"

Sarah leaned close. "I only feed them when they behave. They do like my cooking."

Joann laughed and felt better. "Ah, Sarah, your friendship is good for my soul."

"I cherish your friendship, as well. Who did Otis give your job to?"

"Roman Weaver. I'm to teach him everything I know about the business."

"I see." A thoughtful expression came over Sarah's face. "So you will be working with Roman. Interesting."

"Only until he has learned enough to do my job. What's so interesting about it?"

A gleam entered Sarah's eyes. "Roman is single. You are single."

Joann held up her hand and shook her head. "Oh, no! Don't start matchmaking for me. Roman doesn't know I exist, and it wouldn't matter if he did. I'm not the marrying kind."

"You will be when God sends the right man your way. I'm the perfect example of that. I didn't think I would marry again after my first husband died, but Levi changed my mind. Roman's a nice fellow. Don't let the disappointment of losing your job color your opinion of him."

"I'll try. Just promise me you won't try any of your matchmaking tricks on me."

"No tricks, I promise."

After refusing a ride once more, Joann bid Sarah farewell and glanced again at the lovely little house on the edge of town before heading toward her brother's farm two miles away. Her steps were quicker, but her heart was still heavy.

Roman left his uncle's publishing house and stopped on the narrow sidewalk outside. The realization that he couldn't do the job he loved left him hollow and angry.

He'd never once wanted to work anywhere except in the sawmill alongside his father. The business had been handed down in his family for generations. His mother used to say that he and his father had sawdust in their veins instead of blood. It was close to the truth. Now he was being asked to give it up. The thought was unbearable. He'd already lost so much. He tried not to be bitter, but it was hard.

He wouldn't accept his uncle's offer until he'd had a chance to talk things over with his father. Roman had to know if his father wished this. It hurt to think that he might. The gray clouds gathering overhead matched Roman's mood. Thunder rumbled in the distance.

"What did *Onkel* Otis want?" The question came from Roman's fifteen-year-old brother, Andrew, as he approached from up the street. His arms were full of packages.

"He wanted to see how I'm getting along. Did you find all that *Daed* needed at the hardware store?" He held open the door so his brother could put the parcels on the backseat. The job offer was something he wanted to discuss with his father before he shared the information with Andrew.

"I checked on our order for the new bearings, but they haven't come in yet. I have everything else on father's list."

When Andrew climbed in the front, Roman moved to untie his mother's placid mare from the hitching post. Meg was slow but steady and unlike his spirited gelding, she wouldn't bolt if he lost control of the reins. Managing his high-stepping buggy horse with one arm was just one more thing that he couldn't do anymore.

Maybe his uncle was right. Maybe he should move aside so his father could hire a more able man. It wouldn't be forever.

His parents and Bishop Zook had counseled him to pray for acceptance, but he couldn't find it in his heart to do so. He was angry that God had brought him low in this manner. And for what reason? What had he done to deserve this? Nothing. He climbed awkwardly into the buggy.

"Do you want me to drive?" Andrew asked.

"*Nee,* I can manage." Earlier, Roman had tied the lines together so he could slip them over his neck and shoulder as he often did when he worked behind a team in the fields. That way he couldn't accidently drop the reins. By pulling on first one and then the other, he was able to guide Meg along the street without hitting any of the cars lining the block. Driving still made him nervous. He cringed each time an *Englisch* car sped by, but he was determined to return to a normal life.

Just beyond the edge of town, they passed a woman walking along the road. She carried a green-and-white quilted bag slung over her shoulder. He recognized it as the one that had been hanging from a chair in his uncle's office. This had to be Joann Yoder. He glanced at her face as he passed her and was surprised by the look of dislike that flashed in her green eyes before she dropped her gaze.

What reason did she have to dislike him? The notion disturbed his concentration. He tried to ignore it, but he couldn't.

Dark gray clouds moved across the sky, threatening rain at any moment. Lightning flashed in the distance. The thunder grew louder. He pulled Meg to a stop.

Andrew gave him a quizzical look. "What are you doing?"

"A good deed." He waited.

When the woman came alongside, he touched the brim of his hat. "Would you like a lift?"

"Nee, danki," she replied coldly as she walked past without looking at him.

He studied her straight back and determined walk. If she were this unfriendly, it wouldn't be a joy working with her. Why was she upset with him? He'd rarely even spoken to her.

Roman looked at his brother. "What do you know about Joann Yoder?"

"What is there to know? She's an old *maedel*. She does whatever old maids do. Can we get home? I have chores to do yet this evening, and I'd rather not do them in the dark."

The road ahead was empty. The next farm was over a mile away. A few drops of rain splattered against the buggy top. Roman clicked his tongue to get Meg moving. She plodded down the road until she came even with Joann and then slowed to match the woman's steps. They traveled that way for a few dozen yards. Finally, Joann stopped. The mare did, too.

She smiled as she patted the animal's neck. When she turned toward Roman, her smile vanished. She kept her eyes lowered. He was surprised by a sharp desire to make her look at him again. He wanted to see if her eyes were as green as he thought.

"Did you need something?" she asked.

"*Nee.* We are just on our way home."

"At a snail's pace," Andrew added under his breath.

Roman ignored him. "Allow us to give you a ride. We are obviously going in the same direction. It looks like rain."

"I won't melt."

"But you will be uncomfortable."

"I'll be fine."

"Won't your books get wet?"

She looked down at her bag and back at him. A wary expression flashed across her face. It had been a guess on his part but it appeared he was right about the contents of her bag.

As she stared at him, he saw her eyes *were* an unusual shade of gray-green. They seemed to shift colors according to the light or perhaps her mood. Why hadn't he noticed that about her before now? Maybe because she was always looking down or away. A raindrop struck her cheek and slipped downward like a tear.

For a moment, she didn't say anything, then she nodded and wiped her face. "A lift would be most welcome."

"*Goot*. Where can we take you?" He was ashamed to admit he didn't know where she lived.

"I'm staying with my brother, Hebron Yoder. His farm is just beyond the second hill up ahead."

"We don't go that far," Andrew said under his breath.

"It won't hurt us to go a little out of our way." Roman ignored Andrew's put-upon sigh and waited as Joann rounded the buggy and opened the door on the passenger's side. Maybe he could find out why she disliked him.

Joann wasn't sure what to make of Roman's unusually kind gesture. He'd passed her dozens of times when she was walking along this road without offering her a lift. What was different about today? Did he know she was being fired in order to give him a job? She didn't believe Otis would share that information, but perhaps he had.

Was Roman feeling guilty? If so, then it was up to her to grant forgiveness and get their working relationship off to a good start.

She leaned forward to look around his brother, determined to overcome the shyness that had gotten ahold of her tongue. "Congratulations on your new position."

"What new position?" Andrew demanded.

She caught the annoyed glance Roman flashed at her. She sat back and looked straight ahead. So much for a good start.

"*Onkel* Otis offered me a job at his publishing office," Roman admitted reluctantly.

"Why?" Andrew looked incredulous.

Roman didn't reply. Joann immediately felt sorry for him. The answer was so obvious.

The reason finally dawned on Andrew. "Oh, because of your arm. You didn't take it, did you?"

Joann hadn't considered that possibility. Hope sprang to life in her heart. Was her job safe after all? She waited anxiously for his reply.

"I'm considering it," he said.

Considering meant he hadn't said yes. Was there some way she could convince him to turn down the offer? She had to try. "I'm sure the job wouldn't be to your liking."

"Why do you say that?" he asked.

She racked her mind for a reason. "The work is mostly indoors."

"Not working in the hot sun this summer sounds nice."

She chewed the corner of her lip as she tried to think of another reason he wouldn't want the best job in the world. "It's very noisy when the presses are running."

"I seriously doubt it's noisier than a sawmill." His amusement brought a flush of heat to her face. How silly of her.

All that was left was the truth. She took a deep breath. "It requires hours of reading, excellent comprehension and a firm grasp of writing mechanics as well as an inquisitive mind," she said.

He pulled the mare to a halt and turned to face her. Andrew looked from his brother to Joann and then leaned back out of their way. Roman's brow held a thunderous expression that rivaled the approaching storm. "You don't think I possess those skills?"

She swallowed hard. The truth was the truth. Just because he was upset was no reason to change tactics now. Her chin came up. "I doubt that you do."

"Is that so?"

Joann was tempted to tell him his uncle only offered the job out of pity, but she wisely held her tongue. Nothing good could come from speaking out of spite. She tried to match his stare, but her courage failed. She dropped her gaze to her clenched hands. Why had she started this conversation? It was up to God to decide which one of them was best suited for the job.

In the growing silence, she chanced a glance at Roman's face. His dark expression lightened. Suddenly, he burst out laughing.

"What's so funny?" Andrew asked.

"She's right. I'm not a fellow who enjoys reading or writing."

Joann's hopes rose. "So you don't intend to take the job?"

Roman slapped the reins to get the horse moving. "We'll see. I can learn a new thing if I set my mind to it. Do you always speak so frankly, Joann Yoder?"

Embarrassed, she muttered, "I try not to."

"And why is that?" he asked.

Did he care, or was he trying to make her feel worse? She repeated the phrase her brothers often quoted. "Silence is more attractive than chatter in a woman."

"Says who?" he asked.

"A lot of people."

He wasn't satisfied with her vague answer. "Who, specifically?"

"My brothers," she admitted.

Andrew nodded sagely. "I have to agree."

"I think it depends on the woman," Roman replied.

She glanced at him and thought she caught a glimpse of humor shimmering in his eyes, but she couldn't be sure. Was he laughing at her? Most likely he was. He held her gaze for a long moment before staring ahead again.

Raindrops began splattering against the windshield and roof of the buggy. Joann was every bit as uncomfortable inside as she would've been out in the rain but for a very different reason. Being near Roman made her feel fidgety and on edge, as if something important were about to happen. Thunder cracked overhead and she jumped.

"How long have you worked for our uncle?" Roman asked, looking up at the sky.

"About five months."

"He said that you'll be my teacher if I take the job."

"That's what he told me, too."

"What kind of things would you teach me?"

Andrew interrupted. "I don't know why you're considering it. *Daed* and I need your help in the sawmill. We can't do it all alone."

"I didn't say I was taking it, but I need to know enough to make an informed decision. What things would I have to learn?"

"Many things, like how to set type and run the presses and how to use the binding machines. Eventually, you will have to write articles for the magazine. Many people send us stories to be printed. You'll have to learn how to check any facts that they contain. We don't want to hand out the wrong advice."

"Give me an example."

She thought a moment, and then said, "People send

in home remedies for us to publish in our magazine all the time. Sometimes they are helpful, but sometimes they can be harmful to the wrong person, such as a child. When in doubt, we check with Dr. White or Dr. Zook at the Hope Springs Clinic."

He glanced her way. "Have you written any articles?"

"A few."

"What were they about?"

"I wrote a piece about our history in Hope Springs. I've submitted several tips for the Homemaker Hints section that were published. I've even done a number of poems."

"Interesting. What else would my job entail?"

Andrew rolled his eyes. "I can just see you writing homemaker tips and poetry, *bruder*."

Roman paused a moment, then said, "Roses are red, violets are blue, pine is the cheapest wood, oak is straight and true."

Roman chuckled and smiled at his brother. Andrew grinned and said, "That's not bad. Maybe uncle will use it."

The affection between the two brothers was evident. Joann wished for a moment that she could joke and laugh with her brothers that way. They were all much older than she was. She had come along as a surprise late in her parents' lives. Hebron, the youngest of her brothers, had been fifteen when she was born. They were all married and starting their own families by the time she went to school. Her brothers pretty much ignored her while she was growing up. It was only after their parents died that they decided they knew what was best for her.

Roman clicked his tongue to get Meg to pick up the pace. "Tell me what else I would have to learn."

"You would have to proofread the articles that Otis writes or that others send in to be published. You'll have to attend special meetings in the community in order to report on them, such as the town council meetings and school board meetings. We report the news weekly as well as publish a monthly magazine."

"Sounds like a piece of cake."

"Do you think so?" If he didn't value what they did, how could he do the job well?

When he didn't say more, she leaned forward to glance at him. His face held a pensive look. Was he thinking about taking the job or rejecting it? If only she could tell.

Finally, her brother's lane came into view. By the time they reached the turnoff, the rain had slowed to a few sprinkles. "I'll get out here," she said. "Thanks for the lift."

Roman stopped the buggy. Joann bolted out the door into the gentle rain and hurried toward the house. Once she gained the cover of the front porch, she watched as he turned the buggy around and drove away. At least she could draw a full breath now that she wasn't shut in with him.

What was it about being near him that set her nerves on edge? And how would she be able to work with him day in and day out if he did take the job?

"Please, Lord, let him say no."

Chapter Three

Roman sat at the kitchen table that evening with his parents after supper was done. His conversation with green-eyed Joann earlier that day hadn't helped him come to a decision. He wasn't sure what to do. What would be best for him? What would be best for his family?

Although he lived in the *dawdy-haus,* a small home built next to his parent's home for his grandparents before their passing, he normally took his meals with his family. He waited until his younger brother left the kitchen and his mother was busy at the sink before he cleared his throat and said, "*Daed,* I need to speak to you."

"So speak," his father replied and took another sip of the black coffee in his cup. Menlo Weaver was a man of few words. Roman's mother, Marie Rose, turned away from the sink, dried her hands on a dish towel and joined them at the table. Roman realized as he gazed at her worried face that she had aged in the past months, and he knew he was the reason why.

He took a sip of his own strong, dark coffee. "I spoke with *Onkel* Otis today," he said.

"And?" his mother prompted.

"He offered me a job."

There was no mistaking his father's surprise. Menlo glanced at his wife. She kept her gaze down. Roman knew then that it hadn't been his father's idea. That eased some of his pain. At least his father wasn't pushing to be rid of him.

As always, Menlo spoke slowly, weighing his words carefully. "What was your answer, *sohn?*"

Roman knew his father well. He read the inner struggle going on behind his father's eyes. Menlo didn't want his son to accept the job, but he also wanted what was best for Roman. "I told him I'd think it over."

His mother folded her dish towel on her lap, smoothing each edge repeatedly. "And have you?"

"Of course he's not going to take it," Menlo said.

Roman knew then that he had little choice. His father would keep him on, but the cost to the business would slowly sink it. If Roman had an outside job and brought in additional money for the family, they could afford to hire a strong fellow with two good arms to take his place and make the sawmill profitable again.

He looked his father square in the eye. "I've decided to accept his offer. I hope you understand."

Menlo frowned. "Are you sure this is what you want?"

Roman didn't answer. He couldn't.

"You'll come back to work with me when your arm is better, *ja?*"

Roman smiled to reassure him. "*Ja,* Papa, when my arm gets better."

Menlo nodded. "Then I pray it is a good decision and that you will be healed and working beside me soon."

Roman broached the subject weighing heavily on his

mind. "You will have to hire someone to take my place. Andrew and you can't do it all alone."

"We can manage," his father argued.

"You'll manage better with more help. Ben Lapp is looking for work. He's a fine, strong young man from a good family," his mother countered.

Menlo glanced between his son and his wife. He nodded slowly. "I will speak to him. I thought you were going to tell us you had decided to wed Esta Barkman."

Roman had been dating Esta before the accident. He'd started thinking she might be the one. Since the accident, he'd only taken her home from church a few times. It felt awkward, and he wasn't sure how to act. He didn't feel like a whole man. He avoided looking at his father. "I'm not ready to settle down."

"You're not getting any younger," his mother said. "I'd like grandchildren while I'm still young enough to enjoy them."

"Leave the boy alone. He'll marry soon enough. The supper was *goot*."

"Danki." She smiled at her husband, a warm smile that let Roman know they were still in love. Would Esta smile at him that way after thirty years together? He liked her smile. Her eyes were pale blue, not changeable green, but it didn't matter what color a woman's eyes were. What mattered was how much she cared for him.

He wanted to wait until his arm was healed before asking her to go steady, but his mother was right. He wasn't getting any younger. Now, more than ever, he felt the need to form a normal life.

Menlo finished his coffee and left the room. Roman stayed at the table. His mother rose and came to stand behind him. She wrapped her arms around him and whispered, "I know this is hard for you, but it will all turn out for the best. You'll see."

If only he could believe that. Ever since he was old enough to follow his father into the mill, Roman had known what life held for him. At the moment, it felt as if his life had become a runaway horse and he'd lost the reins. He had no idea where it was taking him. He hated the feeling.

"Are you worried about working for my brother? Otis is a fair man."

"It's not *Onkel* Otis I'm worried about working with. It's his employee, Joann Yoder. She's taken a dislike to me for some reason." It was easier to talk about her than about his self-doubts.

"Nonsense. I can't imagine Joann disliking anyone. She's a nice woman. It's sad that no man has offered for her. She has a fine hand at quilting and a sweet disposition."

"Not so sweet that I've seen."

"She is a little different. According to her sister-in-law, she spends all her time with her nose in a book or out roaming the woods, but it can't be easy for her. Be kind to her, my son."

"What do you mean it can't be easy for her?"

"Joann gets shuffled from one house to another by her brothers. I just meant it can't be easy never having a place to call home."

"I don't understand."

"She's much younger than her brothers. When her parents died, her brothers decided she would spend four months with each of them so as not to burden one family over the other. I honestly believe they think they are being fair and kind. I'm sure they thought she would marry when she was of age, but she hasn't. She's very plain compared to most of our young women."

"She's not that plain." She had remarkable eyes and a pert nose that matched her tart comments earlier that day. Why hadn't he noticed her before? Perhaps because she seldom looked up.

His mother patted his arm. "She's not as pretty as Esta."

"*Nee,* she's not." He rose from the table determined to put Joann Yoder out of his mind. He had much more important things to think about.

"Joann, we're going fishing. Come with us."

Looking up from her book, Joann saw her nieces come sailing through the doorway of the bedroom they shared. Ten-year-old Salome was followed closely by six-year-old Louise.

Joann didn't feel like going out. Truth be told, all she wanted was to sit in her room and pout. Tomorrow they would all travel to Sunday services at the home of Eli Imhoff, and she was sure to see Roman Weaver there. She had no intention of speaking to him.

On Monday, she would learn if she still had her job or if she had lost her chance to buy a home of her own. Last night she prayed to follow God's will, but she really hoped the Lord didn't want Roman to take the job any more than she did. She had tried to find pity in her heart, but the more she thought about him, the less pity entered into the picture. He seemed so strong, so sure of himself. She'd made a fool of herself trying to talk him out of working for Otis.

Why couldn't she stop thinking about him?

Because he was infuriating, that was why. And when

he turned his fierce scowl on her, she wanted to sink through the floor.

"Come on, Papa is waiting for us." Louise pulled at Joann's hand.

She shook her head and said, "I don't think I'll come fishing today, girls."

"You love fishing, *Aenti* Joann. Please come with us," Salome begged.

Louise leaned on the arm of the chair. "What are you reading?"

Joann turned her attention back to her book. She'd read the same page three times now. "It's a wonderful story about an Amish girl who falls in love with the Amish boy next door."

"Does she marry him?" Louise asked.

Joann patted the child's head. "I don't know. I haven't finished the book. I hope she does."

Louise looked up with solemn eyes. "Because you don't want her to be an old *maedel* like you are?"

Joann winced. Out of the mouths of babes.

"That's not nice, Louise," Salome scolded. "You shouldn't call *Aenti* Joann an old maid."

Louise stuck out her bottom lip. "But Papa says she was born to be a *maedel*."

Joann was well aware of her brother's views on the subject of her single status. Perhaps it was time to admit that he was right. A few months ago, she had cherished a secret hope that Levi Beachy would one day notice her. However, Levi only had eyes for Sarah Wyse. The two had wed last Christmas. Joann was happy for them. Clearly, God had chosen them for each other.

Only, it left her without even the faintest prospect for romance. There was no one in Hope Springs that made her heart beat faster.

She closed her book and laid it aside. "Salome, do not scold your sister for speaking the truth."

Joann wanted to know love, to marry and to have children, but if it wasn't to be, she would try hard to accept her lot in life. When did a woman know it was time to give up that dream?

Salome scowled at Louise. Louise stuck her tongue out at her sister and then ran from the room.

Salome turned back to Joann. "It was still a rude thing to say. Never mind that baby. Come fishing with us."

Joann shook her head. "I don't think so."

"But your new fishing pole came. Don't you want to try it out?"

Joann sat up. "It came? When?"

"The mailman brought it yesterday."

"Where is it?"

Salome pointed to the cot in the corner of the upstairs bedroom. "I put it on your bed."

"It's not there now. It wasn't there when I went to bed last night."

"Maybe Louise was playing with it. I told her not to," Salome said, shaking her head.

Joann cringed at the thought. If the younger girl had damaged it, she wouldn't be able to get her money back. She'd foolishly spent an entire week's wages on the graphite rod and open-faced spinning reel combo. In hindsight, it was much too expensive.

Oh, but when she'd tried it out in the store, it cast like a dream. Maybe she should keep it.

No, she gave herself a firm mental shake. She couldn't afford it now. If her hours were cut, she would have to make sacrifices in order to keep putting money in her savings account. Otherwise, she faced a lifetime of moving her cot from one household to another.

Salome dropped to the floor to check under the other beds in the room. Finally, she found it. "Here it is."

Joann breathed a sigh of relief when Salome emerged with the long package intact. Taking the box from her niece, Joann checked it over. It bore several big dents.

"Did she break it?"

"I don't think so." Joann carefully opened one end and slid out the slender black pole. The cork handle felt as light and balanced in her hand now as it had in the sporting goods store. She unpacked the reel. It was in perfect shape.

From the bottom of the stairs, Joann heard her brother call out, "Salome, are you coming?"

"Yes, Papa. Joann is coming, too." She ran out the door and down the stairs.

Joann stared at the pole in her hands. Why not try it out once before sending it back? What could it hurt? It might be ages before she had a chance to use such a fine piece of fishing equipment again. She bundled it into the box, grabbed her small tackle box from beneath her cot, exchanged her white prayer *kapp* for a large black kerchief to cover her head and hurried after her niece.

On her way out of the house, Joann paused long enough to grab an apple from the bowl on the kitchen table. Outside, she joined the others in the back of the farm wagon for the jolting ride along the rough track to a local lake. It wasn't far. Joann walked there frequently, but she enjoyed sitting in the back of the wagon with the giggling and excited girls at her side.

The land surrounding the small lake belonged to an Amish neighbor who didn't care if people fished there as long as they left his sheep alone and closed the gates behind them. Joann had been coming to the lake since she was a child. Joseph Shetler, the landowner, had been friends with her grandfather. The two men often took a lonely little girl fishing with them. Occasionally, Joann still caught sight of Joseph, but he avoided people these days. She never knew why he had become a recluse. He still came to church services, but he didn't stay to visit or to eat.

The wagon bounced and rumbled along the faint wheel tracks that led to the south end of the lake. It had once been a stone quarry that had filled with water nearly a century ago. When they reached the shore, everyone piled out of the back of the wagon and spread out along the water's edge. The remote area was Joann's favorite fishing place. She knew exactly where the large-mouth bass, bluegill and walleye hung out.

She'd spent many happy hours fishing here peacefully by herself, but each time served to remind her of the wonderful days she'd spent there with her grandfather. He had been the one person who always had time for her.

If she closed her eyes, she could still hear his craggy voice. "See that old log sticking out of the bank, child? There's a big bass right at the bottom end of it. Mr. Bass likes to hole up in the roots and dart out to catch unwary minnows swimming by. Make your cast right in front of that log. You'll get him."

Joann smiled at the memory. It had taken many tries and more than a few lost lures before she gained the skill needed to put her hook right where she wanted it. Her *daadi* had been right. She caught a dandy at that spot.

She was always happy when she came to the lake. She kept a small journal in the bottom of her tackle box and made notes about of all her trips. She used the information on weather conditions, insect activity and water temperature to compile information that made her a better angler.

Normally, she released the fish if she was alone. Today, she would keep what she caught and the family would enjoy a fish fry for supper.

When everyone was spreading out along the lakeshore, she said, "I haven't had much success fishing on this end of the lake. The east shore is a better place."

"Looks *goot* to me." Hebron threw in his line.

Joann shrugged and headed away from the lake on a narrow path that wound through the trees for a few hundred yards before it came out at the shore again near a small waterfall. This was where the fishing was the best.

Carefully, she unpacked her pole and assembled it. From her small tackle box, she selected a lure that she knew the walleye would find irresistible and began to cast her line. Within half an hour, she had five nice fish on her stringer.

She pulled the apple from her pocket and bit into the firm, sweet flesh. The sounds of her crunch and of the waterfall covered approaching footsteps. She didn't know she wasn't alone until her brother said, "Joann, I've been calling for you."

Startled, she turned to face him. "I'm sorry, Hebron, I didn't hear you. What do you need?"

"We're getting ready to go. The fish aren't biting today."

"I've been catching lots of walleye. Have you tried a bottom-bouncing lure?" She set her apple beside her on a fallen tree trunk and opened her tackle box to find him a lure like the one she was using.

He waved aside her offering. "I've tried everything. What's that you're fishing with?"

"An orange hopper."

"I meant the rod. Where did you get that?"

She extended her pole for him to see. "I ordered it from the sporting goods store in Millersburg."

"Mighty fancy pole, sister."

"It works wonderfully well. Try casting it, you'll see. You'll be wanting one next."

"My old rod and reel are good enough."

She turned back to the water. "Okay, but I'm the one catching fish."

"Be careful of pride, sister. The *Englisch* world has many things to tempt us away from the true path."

"I hardly think a new fishing pole will make my faith weaker."

"May I see it?" he asked.

"Of course. You can cast twice as far with it as your old one. Give it a try." She handed it over, delighted to show him how well-made it was and how nicely it worked. She picked up her apple and took a second bite.

Hebron turned her rod first one way and then another. "A flashy thing such as this has no place in your life, sister."

"It does if I catch fish for you and your children to eat."

"Are you saying I can't provide for my family?"

"Of course not." She dropped her gaze. Hebron was upset. She could tell by the steely tone creeping into his voice.

He balanced the rod in his hand, nodded and drew back his arm to cast.

Eagerly, she sought his opinion. "Isn't it light? It really is better than any pole I've owned."

He scowled at her, and then threw the rod with all his might. Her beautiful pole spun through the air and splashed into the lake.

"No!" she cried in dismay and took a step toward the water. The apple dropped from her hand.

"False pride goes before a fall, sister," Hebron said. "I would be remiss in my duty if I allowed you to keep such a fancy *Englisch* toy. Already, I see how it has turned your mind from the humble ways an Amish woman should follow. Now, come. We are going home. I will carry your fish. It looks as if God has given us enough to feed everyone after all." With her stringer of fish in his hand, he headed toward the wagon.

She stood for a moment watching the widening ripples where her rod had vanished. Now she had nothing to return and nothing to show for her hard-earned money. Like the chance to own a home, her beautiful rod was gone.

Tears pricked against the back of her eyes, but she refused to let them fall.

Late in the afternoon on Saturday, Roman took off his sling and began the stretching exercises he did every day, four times a day. His arm remained a dead lump, but he could feel an itching sensation near the ball of his shoulder that the doctors assured him was a good sign. As he rubbed the area, the uncomfortable sensation of needles and pins proved that the nerves were beginning to recover. He had been struck by a pickup truck while standing at the side of his buggy on a dark road just before Christmas. The impact sent him flying through the air and tore the nerves in his left shoulder, leaving him with almost complete paralysis in that arm.

Dr. White and Dr. Zook, the local physicians he saw,

were hopeful that he would regain more use of his arm, but they cautioned him that the process would be slow. Unlike a broken bone that would mend in six or eight weeks, the torn nerves in his arm would take months to repair themselves. Even then, there was no guarantee that he would regain the full use of his extremity.

Roman tried to be optimistic. He would work for his uncle until his arm was better. When it was, he would return to working with his father in the sawmill as he had always planned. He held tight to that hope. He had to.

The outside door opened and his brother Andrew came in. He held a pair of fishing poles in one hand. "I'm meeting some of the fellows down at the river for some fishing and a campout. Do you want to come along?"

Roman put his sling back on. He didn't like people seeing the way his arm hung useless at his side. "I don't think so."

"Come on. It will do you good. You used to like fishing."

"I like hunting, I like baseball, I like splitting wood with an ax, but I can't do any of those things. In case you haven't noticed, I've only got one good arm." The bitterness he tried so hard to disguise leaked out in his voice.

"You don't need to bite my head off." Andrew turned away and started to leave.

"Wait. I'm sorry. I didn't mean to snap at you."

Andrew's eyes brightened. "Then you'll come? There's no reason you can't fish with one arm."

"I'm not sure I can even cast a line. Besides, how would I reel in a fish? That takes two hands."

"I've been thinking about that and I have an idea.

It only takes one hand to crank a reel. What you need is a way to hold the rod while you crank. I think this might work."

Andrew opened his coat to reveal a length of plastic pipe hooked to a wide belt and tied down with a strap around his leg.

Roman frowned. "What's that?"

"A rod holder. You cast your line and then put the handle of your pole in this. The inside of the pipe is lined with foam to help hold the rod steady. This way it won't twist while you're cranking. See? I fixed it at an angle to keep the tip of the rod up. All you have to do is step forward or backward to keep tension on the line."

Roman looked at the rig in amazement. "You thought of this yourself?"

It was a clever idea. It might look funny, but the length of pipe held the rod at the perfect angle. "It just might work, little brother," Roman said.

"I know it will. With a little practice, you'll be as good as ever. Come with us." Andrew unbuckled his invention and held it out.

Roman took it, but then laid it on the counter. "Maybe next time."

He didn't want his first efforts to be in front of Andrew and his friends. A child could cast a fishing pole but Roman wasn't sure he could.

Andrew nodded, clearly disappointed. "Yeah, next time," he said.

He left Roman's pole leaning in the corner and walked out. After his brother was gone, Roman stood staring at the rod holder. He picked up his brother's invention. Surely, he could master a simple thing like fishing, even with one arm.

There was only one way to find out. After checking to make sure no one was about, he gathered his rod and left the house. Since he knew Andrew and his friends were going to the river, Roman set off across the cornfield. Beyond the edge of his father's property lay a pasture belonging to Joseph Shetler. Wooly Joe, as he was called, was an elderly and reclusive Amish man who raised sheep.

It took Roman half an hour to reach his destination. As he approached the lake, he saw Carl King, Woolly Joe's hired man, driving the sheep toward the barns. Roman knew Carl wasn't a member of the Amish faith. Like his boss, he kept to himself. The two occasionally came to the mill for wood for fencing or shed repairs, but Roman didn't know them well. When Carl was out of sight, Roman had the lake to himself.

He glanced around once more to make sure he was unobserved. In the fading twilight, he faced the glass-like water that reflected the gold and pink sunset. Lifting his rod, he depressed the button on the reel and cast it out. He hadn't bothered adding bait. He wasn't ready to land a fish and get it off the hook with one hand. Not yet.

He slipped the handle of his rod into the holder his brother had made. It was then he discovered that actually reeling it in wasn't as difficult as he had feared. When he had all the line cranked in, he pulled the rod from the holder and flipped another cast.

This wasn't so bad. Maybe he should have brought some bait. He'd only reeled in a few feet when he felt his hook snag and hang up. He yanked, and it moved a few feet but it wouldn't come free. What was he snagged on?

Chapter Four

Roman discovered just how hard it was to crank his rod with something on the other end. It wasn't a fish, just deadweight. Suddenly, it gave a little more. He half hoped the line would break, but it held. Whatever snagged his hook was being pulled across the bottom of the lake. When he finally managed to wrestle it in, he stared at his prize in amazement. It was someone's fishing pole.

When he stepped down to the water's edge, he noticed a half-eaten apple bobbing at the shoreline. There were fresh footprints in the mud at the edge of the water, too. He'd stumbled upon someone's fishing spot, and they hadn't been gone more than an hour or two.

It was easy to tell that the pole hadn't been in the water long, either. There wasn't a speck of rust on the beautiful spinning reel. The rod and handle were smooth and free of slime.

Whoever had lost the nice tackle had done so recently. Had Carl been fishing before Roman showed up? Was this his pole? It wasn't a run-of-the-mill fishing pole. This was an expensive piece of equipment. Far better than the one Roman owned.

He'd found it. Should he keep it?

He carried his prize to a fallen tree and sat down. It didn't seem right to keep such a high-priced rod and reel. How had it come to be in the lake? Maybe the unfortunate angler had hooked a fish big enough to pull his unattended gear into the water. Whatever happened, Roman was sure the unknown fisherman regretted the loss. He certainly would.

He debated what to do. If he left it here, would the owner return to fish at this spot, or would another angler chance upon it?

He decided on a course of action. From his pocket, he pulled the pencil and small notebook he normally carried to jot down wood measurements. Keeping it handy was a habit.

He wrote: *Fished this nice pole from the lake. Take it if it's yours or you know who owns it.*

That should suffice. He left the pole leaning against the log and weighted his note down with a stone. If the owner returned, it would be here for him. He'd done the right thing. He would check back later in the week. If the rod was still here, then the good Lord wanted him to have it.

Gathering up his old pole, Roman tucked it under his arm and headed for home, content that he'd be able to enjoy an evening of fishing with his brother in the future without embarrassment. At least one thing in his life was looking up. Hopefully, his new job would be just as easy to master.

Joann followed her sister-in-law and her nieces into the home of Eli Imhoff on Sunday morning. She took her place among the unmarried women on the long wooden benches arranged in two rows down the length of the living room. Her cousin, Sally Yoder, sat down beside her.

Sally was a pretty girl with bright red hair, fair skin and a dusting of freckles across her nose. While many thought she was too forward and outspoken, Joann considered her a dear friend. She often wished she could be more like her outgoing cousin. Just behind Sally came Sarah and Levi with Levi's younger sister, Grace. Sarah sat up front with the married women. Grace took a seat on the other side of Joann. Levi crossed the aisle to sit with the men.

Joann's eyes were drawn to the benches near the back on the men's side where the single men and boys sat. She didn't see Roman.

"Are you looking for someone?" Grace asked.

Joann quickly faced the front of the room. "No one special."

"Is Ben Lapp back there?" Sally asked with studied indifference. She picked up a songbook and opened it.

Joann wasn't fooled. Sally was head over heels for the handsome young farmer. Ben was the only one who didn't seem to know it.

Joann glanced back and saw where Ben was sitting just as Roman came in and took a seat. Their eyes met, and she quickly looked forward again. She whispered to Sally, "Ben is here."

"Is he looking at me?"

"How should I know?"

"Check and see if he's looking this way."

Joann glanced back. Ben wasn't looking their way, but Roman was. Joann quickly faced forward and opened her songbook.

Sally nudged her with her elbow. "Well? Is he?"

"No."

"Oh." Disappointed, Sally snapped her book closed. After a moment, she leaned close to Joann. "Is he looking now?"

"I'm not going to keep twisting my head around like a curious turkey. If he's looking, he's looking. If he isn't, he isn't."

"Fine. What's wrong with you today?"

"I'm sorry. I'm just upset because I may lose my job."

"Why? What happened?" Grace asked.

"Otis wants his nephew to take over my position."

Sally gave up trying to see what Ben was doing. "Which nephew?"

"Roman Weaver."

Grace shot her a puzzled look. "What does Roman know about the printing business?"

"Whatever I can teach him in two weeks. After that, I go back to my old job at the bookstore. Oh, I'm the cleaning lady now, too."

"That's not fair," Sally declared. "You do a wonderful job for the paper. My mother says the *Family Hour* magazine has been much more interesting since you started working for Otis."

Joann sighed. "I love the job, but what can I do?"

"Quit," Sally stated as if that solved everything. "Tell Otis he can train his own help and clean his own floors."

"You know I can't do that. I need whatever work I can get."

Esta Bowman came in with her family. Grace nodded slightly to acknowledge her. Esta moved forward to sit on a bench several rows in front of Sally. The two women had been cool toward each other for months.

According to gossip, Esta had tried to come between Grace and her come-calling friend, Henry Zook. Happily, she had failed. Grace confided to Sally that she and Henry would marry in the fall. Although Amish betrothals were normally kept secret, Sally shared the news with Sarah and Joann. Joann hadn't told anyone else.

Grace whispered to her. "Esta has been at it again. Everyone knows she's walking out with Roman Weaver, but according to her sister, she's just doing it to make Faron Martin jealous. Two weeks ago, Henry saw her kissing Ben Lapp."

"Ben wouldn't do that," Sally snapped.

Grace waved aside Sally's objection. "I think she was only trying to make Faron notice her. Anyway, it worked. She left the barn party last Saturday with Faron, and I saw them kissing. I noticed he drove his courting buggy today. Mark my words, she'll ride home with him this evening and not with Roman."

Joann discovered she wanted to hear more about Roman's romantic attachment, but she knew church wasn't the place to engage in gossip. She softly reminded Grace of that fact. Grace rolled her eyes but fell silent.

Joann resisted the urge to look back and see if Roman's gaze rested tenderly on Esta. It was none of her business if he was about to be dumped by a fickle woman.

Joann turned her heart and mind toward listening to God's word.

After the church service, the families gathered for the noon meal and clustered together in groups to catch up on the latest news. There were two new babies to admire and newlyweds to tease. Then Moses and Atlee Beachy got up a game of volleyball for the young people that kept everyone entertained. It was pleasant to visit with the friends she didn't see often. Joann was sorry when it came time to leave. She found herself searching for Roman in the groups of men still clustered near the barn but didn't see him. Nor did she see Esta among the women.

Hebron walked up to her, a scowl on his face. "Have you seen the girls?"

She looked around for her nieces. "I think they were playing hide-and-seek in the barn with some of the other children."

"See if you can find them. I'm ready to go."

Joann walked into the barn in search of her nieces. It wouldn't be the first time the girls had stayed hidden to keep from having to go home when they were having fun. They often played this game. After calling them several times, Joann accepted that she would have to join the game and find them herself. She climbed the ladder to the hayloft. A quick check around convinced her they weren't hiding there. So where were they?

Joann returned to the ground level and began checking in each of the stalls. She didn't believe the girls would be hiding with any of the horses, but she didn't know where else to look. One stall was empty. A rustling sound from within caught Joann's attention. She stepped inside but her search only turned up a cat with a litter of kittens curled up in a pile of straw in the far corner. She took a moment to reassure the new mother. Stepping closer, she stooped to pet the cat and admire the five small balls of black-and-white fur curled together at her side. It was then she heard Roman's voice. "Esta, I wish to speak to you alone."

"You sound so serious, Roman. What's the matter?"

"May I speak frankly?" Something in his voice held Joann rooted to the spot.

"Of course. We're friends, aren't we?"

"I hope that we have become more than friends. That's what I wish to talk about."

"Why, Roman, I'm not sure I know what you mean." Esta's coy reply sent Joann's heart to her feet. She needed to let them know she was present, but she dreaded facing Roman. Maybe if she stayed quiet, they would leave and she wouldn't be discovered. She held her breath and prayed. To her dismay, they stopped right outside the stall where she crouched beside the kittens.

"Can I take you home tonight?" Roman asked.

"Did you bring your courting buggy? I thought you came with your family."

"I did come with my family, but it would make me very happy if you would walk out with me this evening."

"I've already told Faron Martin that he could take me home. He brought his courting buggy."

"Tell him you've changed your mind."

"But I haven't."

"Esta, don't do this to me."

"Don't do what? I want to ride in Faron's buggy. He's got a radio in it, and his horse is a mighty flashy stepper. Almost as pretty as your horse, but of course, you can't drive him anymore, can you?"

Joann heard the teasing in Esta's voice. She was toying with Roman. Did she care who took her home as long as they had a tricked-out buggy? Joann wanted to shake her. How could a woman be so fickle?

"Esta, I'm ready to settle down. Aren't you?"

"Are you serious?"

"Very serious."

Joann wished she was anywhere else but eavesdropping on a private conversation. She shouldn't be listening. She covered her ears with her hands and took a step back. She didn't know the mother cat had moved behind her until she stepped on her paw.

The cat yowled and sank her teeth into Joann's leg.

She shrieked and shook the cat loose as she stumbled backward. She lost her balance and hit the stall door. The unlatched gate flew open and Joann found herself sprawled on her backside at Roman's feet.

Esta began laughing, but there was no mirth on Roman's face.

"What do you think you're doing?" he demanded.

"I'm sorry," she sputtered, struggling to her feet.

Esta crossed her arms. "She's making a fool of herself, as usual."

"I was looking for my nieces, if you must know." Joann said as she dusted off her skirt and straightened her *kapp*.

A smug smile curved Esta's lips. "She's just eavesdropping on us because she can't get a boyfriend of her own."

Joann's chin came up. "At least I don't go around kissing everyone who walks out with me."

Shock replaced Esta's grin. "How dare you."

Growing bolder, Joann took a step closer. "Which one is a better kisser? Ben Lapp or Faron Martin?"

"Oh!" Esta's face grew beet red. She covered her cheeks with her hands and fled.

It was Joann's turn to sport a smug grin. It died the second she caught sight of Roman's face. The thunderous expression she dreaded was back.

"What have I ever done to you?" he asked in a voice that was dead calm.

She looked down, unable to meet his gaze. "Nothing."

"Then why your spiteful behavior?"

"You call the truth spiteful?" She glanced up, trying to judge his reaction.

"What truth is that?"

"Esta Barkman is a flirt, and she's using you."

"I won't listen to you speak ill of her."

"Suit yourself." She swept past him, wishing that she had kept her mouth closed. What did she care if Esta was leading him on? It was none of her business what woman he cared for. Joann only hoped she had opened his eyes to Esta's less-than-sterling behavior even if it cost his good opinion of her.

On Monday morning, a faint hope still flickered in Joann's heart as she walked up to the front door of the publishing office. She didn't see Roman's buggy on the street. Perhaps he wouldn't come, and she could continue with her job as if nothing had happened. Oh, how she prayed that was God's will.

She paused with her hand on the doorknob. "Please, Lord, don't make me work with that man," she whispered.

She pushed open the door and came face-to-face with the object of her prayers. Roman Weaver stood behind the front counter. He scowled at her and glanced over his shoulder at the clock on the wall. It showed five minutes past nine. Looking back at her, he said, "You're late."

Great. Just great. He was here in spite of her prayers. This was going to be a long day.

Joann hung her bag on the row of pegs beside the door as she struggled to hide her disappointment. "I'm not late. That clock is ten minutes fast. I've been meaning to reset it. Welcome to Miller Press. We publish a monthly correspondent magazine with reports from scribes in a number of Amish settlements, plus other news and stories. We also publish a weekly paper that has sections on weddings, births, deaths, accidents and other special columns. Besides those two, we also do custom print jobs."

Two straw hats hung on the pegs. That meant only Otis and Roman had come in. Gerald Troyer and Leonard Jenks would be in anytime now. Hopefully they would come quickly. She was running out of things to say.

The thought no sooner crossed her mind than the outside door opened and Gerald walked in. A tall and lanky young man, his short, fuzzy red-brown beard proclaimed him a newlywed. "Morning, Joann. Did you have a nice weekend?"

"Well enough. And you?" She refused to look at Roman. She would need to apologize at some point for her behavior yesterday.

Although he was Amish, Gerald belonged to a congregation from a neighboring town. He sighed heavily. "My wife's family came for a surprise visit."

"And how did that go?" Joann asked.

"Her mother is nice enough, but I don't think her father likes me. He didn't say more than four words to me the entire weekend."

She saw him glance pointedly at Roman. She couldn't delay the moment any longer. She gestured toward Roman. "Gerald, this is Roman Weaver. Roman is going to be working with us."

"Excellent. Are you a pressman, reporter or typesetter?" Gerald asked as he held out his hand.

Roman shook it. "None of those, I'm afraid, but I'm willing to learn."

Joann said, "Otis wants Roman to learn all aspects of the business. Gerald is our typesetter and helps with local news reporting."

"Minding my p's and q's, that's me," Gerald said with a wide grin.

Joann noticed the puzzled look Roman gave him. He really didn't know anything about the business. She explained. "All type is set in reverse so that when it's printed it's in the correct position. The p and the q look so much alike that it is easy to mix them up. Typesetters have to mind their p's and q's. It's a very old joke."

Roman didn't look amused. "I see. Minding my p's and q's is my first lesson. What's next, teacher?"

He stressed the last word. To Joann's ears it almost sounded like an insult. Any hope of a good working relationship between them was fading fast.

"I guess we'll start with the layout of the building."

She indicated the high front counter with a tall chair behind it. "The business consists of six separate spaces. Here in the front office, we take orders for printing jobs, accept information and announcements for the paper and take payments for completed orders."

Otis had his office door closed so she knew not to disturb him. "To the left is your uncle's office. Otis oversees all aspects of the business. Any questions I can't answer, he'll be able to."

The front door opened again and a small, elderly gray-haired man entered. He wore faded blue jeans and a red plaid shirt with the sleeves rolled up. His fingernails were stained with ink. He nodded to Joann.

"Leonard Jenks, I'd like you to meet Roman Weaver," she said.

"You're Otis's nephew, aren't you? He told me he offered you a job. Don't expect special treatment."

"I don't," Roman replied, meeting the man's gaze with a steady one of his own.

Leonard nodded, and then said, "Once I get the generator started, we can run those auction handbills. You have them ready, right Joann?"

"I need to put one through the proof press before we get started. I wanted to wait and show Roman how that's done."

"Then you'd best get to it. Make sure he knows I won't waste my time and my eyesight trying to read his chicken scratching. Block print every order," Leonard said, then crossed to a door at the back of the room and went out.

"Friendly fellow," Roman said.

"You have to give him a chance to get to know you. As he mentioned, no one uses cursive writing here. Everything must be printed legibly. Anything you've written that you want to go into print must be typed up. Can you type?"

He arched one eyebrow. "No."

Joann could have kicked herself. Of course he couldn't type with just one hand. She rushed on to cover her mistake. "Leonard's wife will type up your work. Just let Otis know when you need her."

"I'll learn how to do it. I'm surprised to see an *Englisch* fellow working here. I thought they all went in for computer printing these days."

"Leonard worked for fifty years at a printing company in Cleveland. When they upgraded to more modern presses, he found himself out of a job. Your uncle purchased their old equipment. When Leonard learned where the equipment was going, he asked Otis for a job and moved to Hope Springs. He's invaluable. He knows the equipment inside and out and he can fix anything that goes wrong."

"Is that why his unsociable behavior is tolerated?"

"In part. As I was saying, these are the front offices.

Through this door is the makeup room and the table where the type is kept along with our proof press."

She opened the door and went in. Gerald was putting on a large leather apron. "I'll show you how type setup works when Joann is finished with you," he said to Roman.

The sooner she was finished with him the better. Having Roman following her was like having a surly dog at her back. She expected him to snap at her at any second. Her nerves were stretched to the breaking point.

Should she apologize for her comments yesterday or should she go on as if nothing had happened? She certainly wasn't about to mention their meeting in front of Gerald.

"Next door to this building is a bookshop where our books are available to the public," she said. "The store is run by Mabel Jenks, Leonard's wife."

"My uncle hired the wife, too? That's surprising."

"She isn't an employee. He sold half the bookstore to her. Your uncle's business needed to expand beyond the borders of this town. He had books and pamphlets for sale in the store as well as a library of important Amish works. Many are quite rare. Selling part of the bookstore to Mabel, an *Englisch* partner, allowed Otis to expand to the internet so that people from all over the world could find information about the Amish and search for our books. Mabel runs our website, too."

"I had no idea this was such a big operation."

At least he finally seemed impressed with something she was showing him. "Beyond this setup room are the presses. We have four. You'll learn to run each one."

"Leonard will show me that?"

"Ja."

"I can hardly wait."

She ignored his sarcasm. "In keeping with the *Ordnung* of our Amish congregation, we don't use electricity. The lamps are gas. A diesel generator that sits behind the building runs the equipment that isn't hand-operated. It's Leonard's baby, but he'll show you what to do in case you have to run it in a pinch."

"I took a look at them earlier. They're the same type we use at our sawmill."

"I'm glad you're familiar with them." At least he was qualified to do something at his uncle's business.

She wasn't sure why he had accepted the position. She'd never met anyone less suited to become an editor and office manager, a job that fit her like a glove. Somehow, she was going to have to get him up to speed and quickly. If she couldn't, would Otis let her stay? She doubted it. He was getting on in years. Was he thinking about who would take over after he was gone? If he wanted it to be his nephew, well, she understood, but she didn't have to like it.

She kept walking with Roman close on her heels as they passed between the presses. Hopefully, Otis would want Roman to spend the rest of the day with him or with Leonard. She was going to be a nervous wreck if he was breathing down her neck all day.

"Back here is our storage room." She opened the door and stepped inside. Roman followed.

She'd never noticed how small the room was until he took up all the available space and air. "We keep paper, solvents for cleaning ink off the type and such in here along with rolls of wire for our binder," she said breathlessly. "I'll give you a list of what we stock and how to find it."

"All right."

She turned to face him and gathered her courage. "That's the grand tour. Any questions?"

"Not really." He leaned casually against the door-jamb blocking her only exit.

Now what should she do?

Chapter Five

Her voice held a funny quality that Roman couldn't quite identify. Was it resentment, fear or something else? Before he could decide, she clasped her hands together and said, "About yesterday."

He wondered if she would bring it up. She had spoiled more than his opportunity to take Esta home. He had doubts now that hadn't existed before. What if she was telling the truth? Did he want to know?

"What about yesterday?"

"I want to apologize."

"For what?"

She stared at the floor. "You know."

"I'm not sure I do. Why don't you explain." He couldn't help the amusement that crept into his voice. It wouldn't hurt her to squirm a little before he forgave her. She had been rude to Esta. Although, he had to admit Esta shared part of the blame for the exchange.

He almost missed the baleful glare Joann flashed at him before she looked down at her hands. No wonder she didn't look up often. She gave herself away when she did. Those green eyes of hers reflected her emotions the way still waters reflected the sky and clouds overhead.

"I'm sorry I didn't announce myself when I realized you were having a private conversation," she said. "I should have."

"And?" he prompted.

"And I shouldn't have said those things to Esta," she added in a rush. She tried to move past him, but he continued blocking the doorway.

"And?"

The color rose in her cheeks, making them glow bright pink. He wanted to see how far he could push before that outspoken streak she tried so hard to curtail came out. He didn't have to wait long.

Her gaze snapped up and locked with his. Sparks glittered in the depths of her eyes. "And I'm sorry it was all true!"

He struggled not to smile, having gotten the reaction he wanted. "That's hardly an apology."

Her eyes narrowed as she glared at him. "It's all you're going to get. Your uncle hired you to work here. Don't you think you should get started?"

Roman stepped out of the door and swept his arm aside to indicate she should go first. She hesitated, then squeezed past him. He caught a whiff of a pleasing floral scent. Roses maybe. It had to be from her shampoo or soap. Amish women didn't wear perfumes. Whatever it was, he liked it.

She marched ahead of him to the front of the office. His uncle was behind the front counter waiting on a customer. He called Roman over and showed him the price list they used for ads and single-page flyers and posters. It was easy enough to understand. When the customer left, Otis asked, "How is your first day going?"

Roman lowered his voice. "Joann doesn't seem happy to have me here."

Otis frowned as he looked around Roman to where Joann was gathering a stack of papers from her desk. "Has she said something to that effect? I'll speak to her if she has been rude."

"No, it's probably just me."

"All right, but let me know if she or anyone makes you feel unwelcome. This is my shop, and I say who works here."

Joann crossed the room to join them with several letters clutched to her chest. Her smile was stiff. "Are you ready to learn how to use the proof press?"

"Absolutely, teacher. Lead on."

Her smile stayed in place, but he knew she was annoyed by his pet name for her. All she said was, "Please follow me."

Her instructions were precise and to the point. She quickly showed him how to operate the small press that made a single copy of the handbill they were doing. She handed the first printed page to him. "Read it over and look for mistakes. If you have set the type, get someone else to read it. Errors can slip by because you read it knowing what it should say instead of what is actually on paper."

He scanned the paper carefully and immediately spotted a misspelling. "This should be 'working baler' not 'woking baler,' unless someone does bale woks, whatever that would be."

She frowned at him and leaned close to examine the paper in his hand. Again, he caught the fresh scent of flowers. She glanced up at him and quickly moved a step away. "You're right. I'll let Gerald know. Once he has corrected the letters in the composition stick, we'll turn the project over to Leonard. He'll print the size and number of handbills that were ordered."

"Okay, teacher, what's next?"

He caught a glimpse of the sparks that flashed in her green eyes again before she looked away. With deliberate calm, she said, "The mail. We'll go through it and sort it into letters for the newspaper, ones that might go in the magazine and those that need Otis's attention."

She strode toward the front of the building, and he followed, amused by the square set of her shoulders and intrigued by the gentle sway of her hips.

That thought brought him up short. She had done nothing but cause trouble for him. The last thing he expected was to find her attractive in any way. He quickly dismissed his reaction and focused on what she was saying.

She indicated a stack of mail and offered him a letter opener. She read the first letter. "Alma Stroltzfus is going to be one hundred years old on the twenty-fifth of this month. Her family is hosting a get-together in honor of the day. Family from all across the state will be there. This should go in the weekly paper. Our magazine doesn't come out until after the date, but we could mention it there, too."

He opened his first letter. "This is from a farmer on Bent Tree Road. He is offering forgiveness to the youth who set fire to his haystacks. Magazine or newspaper?"

"Newspaper, I think." She opened the next letter. "This is a poem about losing a child and dealing with that grief. Definitely a piece for the magazine."

They both reached for the stack of mail at the same time. Their hands touched. She jerked away as if he were a hot stove, her eyes wide with shock. "We can finish this later. Let's have Gerald show you how to set type."

As she hurried away, he noticed again the soft curve of her hips beneath her faded dress. There was definitely more to Joann Yoder than met the eye.

By noon, Roman's head was spinning with all the information Joann poured onto him like syrup over a stack of hotcakes. Some of it was soaking in, but a great deal of it slid off his brain and pooled around his feet. He had no idea there was so much to his uncle's business. He hated to admit it, but he was impressed by Joann's scope of knowledge.

There had been a steady stream of customers into the shop all morning. Some placed orders, but many stopped in simply to leave notices and announcements to run in the paper. Joann took care of the customers, accepted payments, filed the notes and continued to serve him a steady diet of information about what his work would entail.

This wasn't going to be an easy job to master. It wasn't one job. There were dozens of new skills he'd have to learn. He clung tight to the thought that if a woman could manage the place so easily after only five months, then so could he.

Otis came out of his office and said, "Time for lunch."

Joann went to the front door and turned the open sign to closed. Below it, she hung a second sign that said they would return at one o'clock.

"Roman, you are welcome to come home with me. My wife would be delighted to feed you," Otis said.

"I'm sorry, I can't join you today. I have an appointment with Doctor Zook. Please tell *Aenti* Velda I'll be happy to eat with you tomorrow."

"I'll do that. I go right by the clinic on my way home. I'll walk with you." He settled his hat on his head and held open the door. Roman grabbed his own straw hat from the peg and stepped out ahead of him.

As they walked side by side on the narrow sidewalk, they passed a few buggies and cars parked alike in front of the various businesses. It was Monday, and quiet in the small village that nestled amid the farms and pastures of rural Ohio. The main activity seemed to be near the end of the street. Roman noticed his mother's cart parked outside a shop.

Otis asked, "Well, what do you think?"

"I think there is a lot to know."

Otis chuckled. "I do more than shuffle papers all day."

"I'm learning that. It's sure not what I expected."

They stepped aside to let a group of women pass in front of them. They were headed into the fabric shop. Roman caught sight of his mother through the window. Otis saw her, too, and waved. She smiled brightly and waved back.

Otis said, "I see the ad and flyers I printed for the big sale today at Needles and Pins are bringing in customers. That's good. That will mean repeat business."

Roman looked at his uncle. "What made you start a printing shop? Your father ran a dairy farm, didn't he?"

"*Ja.* I worked on the farm with my brothers, but I saw a need among our people for decent things to read. There was a series of articles in one of the local newspapers by an unhappy ex-Amish fellow who believed his new ways were better, and he urged others to follow them."

"We face that all the time. Our life is not for everyone."

"True, but a man must be careful what he reads. Without meaning to, he can allow unholy thoughts to take root in his mind. I started thinking about getting a small press because of those writings and because a friend told me about an old Amish book he wanted to see reprinted. My brother and I printed the book in our barn. It was no thing of beauty, but people bought copies. Not long after that, a woman I knew wrote a manuscript and she asked our Bishop how she might get it published. The Bishop sent her to me. I soon realized the Lord was nudging me to start a business where good Amish folks could find appropriate reading material."

"You print more than books now."

Otis smiled and nodded. "That we do. The magazine grew out of letters people wrote to us after reading some of our books. Once the magazine became popular, people wanted to read the news about their Amish neighbors every week instead of once a month. I bought a bigger press and hired people to help me. Running the press only one day each week wasn't cost-efficient so we started printing flyers, pamphlets and advertisements."

"Not everyone who came in today was Amish."

"We do work for *Englisch* customers as long as the content is acceptable according to our ways. We now print schoolbooks and cookbooks, too. Tourists love our Amish cookbooks. I truly believe the good Lord has caused my business to prosper because I stayed true to His teachings."

"You have created a fine thing, uncle."

"No more than your father has done. Men need good solid wood to build strong houses and barns. I believe we also need good solid books to build strong minds."

They had come to the corner in front of the Hope

Springs Medical Clinic. Otis walked on toward his home and a hot lunch while Roman entered the waiting room of the clinic. His uncle's words about good books stayed in his mind. Roman had always considered reading to be something he needed to get by in business and for church. He'd never thought of it as a way to improve his mind.

His father led the family in prayers and Bible reading each morning and evening. Roman read the Bible sometimes at night, but not as often as he should. He wondered what books his uncle would suggest he read. He would make a point to ask him. The thought of books brought Joann to mind. What did she like to read?

He shook his head. Why was he thinking about her, again? She was like a cocklebur stuck to his sock. Not exactly painful, but irritating and difficult to get rid of.

Fortunately, his name was called, and Roman followed the nurse back to a small exam room. Dr. Zook came in a few moments later. Roman waited quietly as he read his chart.

He looked up at last. "I received a letter from the neurosurgeon that did your surgery," Dr. Zook said. "He's optimistic about your recovery."

"I'm glad one of us is."

Dr. Zook closed the chart. "He believes with therapy you should recover some of your hand functions."

"Some, but not all?"

"Are you doing your exercises regularly?"

"*Ja,* but I still can't move my arm."

"I'm not surprised. Brachial plexus injuries such as the one you sustained take a long time to heal. Nerves grow very slowly. Only a fraction of an inch in a month. It may be a few months to a few years before your recovery is complete."

"No one will tell me if I'll be able to use my arm again. Will I?"

"We simply don't know. The brachial plexus, the network of nerves that carry signals from your spine to your shoulder, arm and hand, was badly damaged. Two of your nerves were torn apart. While the surgeon was able to repair them, we're not sure they will function as they once did. Other nerves were stretched drastically when that pickup hit you. It was a blessing you weren't killed."

"Somehow, this doesn't feel like a blessing."

Dr. Zook rose and helped Roman remove his sling. He examined the arm, moving it gently. "Have you noticed any changes at all?"

"I've had some twitches in my forearm."

"That's good. As the nerves start to regrow, you'll feel twitching in the muscles they supply. We can start specific exercises to improve those muscles when it happens. Keep up with your stretches. It's important to keep your joints limber. Once they freeze, there isn't much that can be done for them. How is the pain?"

"Always there."

"Have the pills I've given you helped at all?"

"Some. Keeping my mind occupied helps, too."

"I wish there was more I could do to help, but it is going to take time and it's going to be painful."

"So I've been told."

"I want you to be very careful at work. You could injure your arm badly and never feel it. A sawmill can be a dangerous place at the best of times."

Roman slipped his arm back in the sling. "I'm not working at the mill right now."

"Oh?"

"I'm working at my uncle's print shop."

"That's good. While it may be less physically demanding there, it has its own set of dangers. I've bandaged a few crushed fingers and put some stitches in your uncle, too. Just remember to pay attention."

"I will."

"This injury was life-changing for you, Roman. It can't be easy making the adjustments you've had to make. How are the flashbacks?"

"Less frequent."

"Are you sleeping okay?"

"Sometimes."

"Nightmares?"

"Sometimes."

"Roman, depression is natural after an injury like yours. Anger and sadness are symptoms that can be treated if they persist. Don't be afraid to tell me if you have that kind of trouble."

"It was God's will. I must accept that."

"I believe everything happens for a reason, and that God has a plan for everyone, but He invented doctors to help people along the way. So let me do my job, okay? I'll see you in two weeks or sooner if you need me." The young doctor smiled and left the room.

Roman saw no reason to smile. He was crippled, and no one could tell him when, or if, he would recover.

Joann jumped when the front door banged open, but it wasn't Roman returning. It was only her cousin, Sally.

"Hi, Joann. I brought the sketches that Otis wanted. Is he here?" Sally's cheerful face never failed to brighten Joann's day. Her talent as an artist was well known in the community, and she often supplied the black-and-white line drawings that were the only graphics used in the *Family Hour* magazine. Otis would give her a list of things he wanted for the next month's layout and what size they should be. Her beautifully drawn images of ordinary Amish life never failed to amaze Joann.

"Otis isn't back from lunch yet. Can you wait for him?"

"Sure. I've already done my shopping. I got the prettiest lilac material at Needles and Pins for half off. You should get over there and get some. It's going fast."

"I don't have need of a new dress. Mine are fine."

"They may be fine as you see it, but they are getting a little threadbare and stained. Besides, that gray isn't your best color."

Joann looked down at her dress and matching apron. It was an old dress, but it was comfortable. "I like it because it doesn't show the ink stains so readily."

"I'm just saying it wouldn't hurt to take a little more care with your appearance. You might have the chance to impress a fine fellow who comes in to place an ad," Sally said.

What did Roman think of her attire? Why should he think of her at all? Deciding it was time to change the subject, Joann reached for the folder her cousin held. "May I see your sketches?"

Sally beamed. "I was hoping you'd ask."

After laying the sketches side by side on the countertop, Sally shifted her gaze to Joann. "Do you think these are what Otis had in mind?"

The outside door opened, and Roman entered the shop with a deep frown creasing his forehead. Had the doctor given him bad news? "I hope he feels bad about taking your job," Sally whispered to Joann as she gave him a cool stare.

Joann gripped Sally's arm and said under her breath, "Please don't say anything."

Fortunately, Gerald came out of the typesetting room at that moment. "Sally, have you brought us some more of your artwork?"

"I brought in four pieces to see if this is what Otis wanted."

"He should be back any minute. Let's see what you have. Roman, Sally is our artist. She can draw almost anything."

Sally blushed. "I have a small talent."

Gerald moved to stand beside the women. Roman hesitated, as if unsure what to do. Joann said, "Come look at these, Roman, and tell us what you think."

He came forward and studied the array. "They're nice. I like this one best."

"I do, too." Joann held up the sketch of a small girl handing her mother jars from a basket.

"It reminds me of my mother's storeroom in the cellar," he said. "She has hundreds of jars on her shelves."

Sally nodded. "I sketched it while my mother was helping my sister put up green beans last summer. The little girl was inspired by my niece."

"It's darling, Sally," Joann said. "I hope Otis will use it on the cover of the next issue. He's writing a series of articles about stewardship. What a great way to show people how being good stewards is really a part of everyday life."

"I didn't know if he would object to the partial view of the child's face. I know some of your customers belong to more conservative churches."

Joann studied the picture closely. Sally had been careful to draw the woman's figure from the back so that her face wasn't seen, but the child had been sketched in profile.

"I think it's fine. What do you men think?"

"Looks good to me," Gerald said.

"If it's controversial, I say don't use it," Roman added his two cents.

Joann saw the joy go out of Sally's eyes. Roman didn't realize how much Sally's artwork meant to her. She never signed her work or took credit for doing it, but she wanted to use the talent God had given her to glorify Him. This was her way of doing that.

"Otis has the final say," Joann said. "It's up to him."

Otis returned a few minutes later. He looked over Sally's sketches and agreed with Joann's assessment. Thankfully, he kept Roman with him the rest of the afternoon, and Joann had a chance to relax. Roman left a few minutes before five. Joann stayed behind to tidy up the shop.

When she left the building, she was surprised to see Roman come out of the bookstore next door. He had two novels tucked inside his sling. He paused when he caught sight of her. After a moment of hesitation, he said, "My buggy is just around the corner. Would you care to share a ride?"

There wasn't a cloud in the sky. He had no reason to offer her a lift today. "It doesn't look like rain."

"I thought since we were going the same way…" His voice trailed off. He cocked an eyebrow and waited.

It was a long walk after a long day, but she'd rather crawl home on her hands and knees than spend another minute in his company. Thankfully, she managed not to blurt out her opinion. "I have errands to run. I'll see you tomorrow."

Tomorrow would arrive all too quickly.

"Suit yourself." Without another word, he walked away and turned the corner.

Had he actually sounded disappointed? She couldn't

imagine why unless he'd come up with a new way to torment her and wanted to test it out.

She started walking, determined not to look back. She was being unkind, but the thought of spending the next two weeks showing him how to do her job was almost more than she could bear. She wasn't herself when he was near. She had to be careful not to trip on her words or run into a desk. He made her feel awkward and jumpy and she had no idea why.

The sad part was that her two weeks with him wouldn't be the end of it. She'd still be coming in to clean. Would he ask why she'd changed jobs? Or why she was cleaning when she knew so much about printing? What would she say?

The answer to those questions would have to wait. There was no sense worrying about it before it happened.

She did have an errand to run. It hadn't been just an excuse. She stopped at the public library to inquire if the latest copy of *Ohio Angler* had come in. It hadn't.

The *Angler* was the one *Englisch* magazine that she read cover to cover. She suspected that her brothers wouldn't approve, so she never checked it out. She simply read it at the library. It was from those glossy pages that she had gleaned much of her knowledge about fishing. That and spending hours and hours with a pole in her hand.

Disappointed, she left the library and walked through town toward her brother's home. She passed Sarah's house without stopping. That dream was over. She would just have to learn to accept it. When she reached the lane to her brother's farm, she stopped. She didn't feel like going home yet. She needed to be alone and think. She needed the solace of the lake.

Chapter Six

Roman's spirits lifted when he walked into his mother's kitchen. The wonderful aromas of baking ham, scalloped potatoes and hot dinner rolls promised a delicious meal would soon be ready. His mother, with beads of sweat on her upper lip, was stirring applesauce in a large pan on the stove.

She looked over at him and smiled. "You're just in time. Your papa has gone to wash up. How was it? Was Otis kind to you?"

"It was fine. I'll go wash up, too. Where is Andrew?" His bottomless pit of a brother was always in the kitchen trying to sneak a bite of this or that before his mother got it on the table.

A worried frown creased her brow. "He said he wasn't hungry."

Roman stared at her in shock. "Andrew said that? He must be sick."

Roman's father came into the room. "He's not sick. He just doesn't like change. Can't say that I do, either."

"We change when we must," Marie Rose stated quickly. "It's ready. Have a seat." She opened the door of the oven and pulled out the ham.

Roman could tell his father wanted to say more, but he simply took his place at the head of the table.

Marie Rose scowled at Roman. "Go wash up. Don't make your father wait on you."

Joann rounded the bend in the narrow path that led to her favorite spot at the lake and stopped dead in her tracks. A fishing pole, exactly like her new one her brother had thrown into the water, was leaning against a log where she liked to sit. She glanced around expecting to see another angler, but there was no one in sight. She called out, but no one answered.

The breeze off the water caused a bit of paper on the log to flutter. She moved closer and saw the paper had been weighted down with the stone. Picking it up, she read the note and her heart gave a happy leap. It wasn't a pole like hers. It was hers.

By the grace of God, someone had snagged her pole and pulled it from the depths of the lake. She hugged the note to her chest as she spun around with joy.

"Oh, thank you, thank you, thank you," she shouted. If only the unknown angler were present, she would thank him or her in person.

As quickly as her elation bubbled up, it ebbed away. She had her pole back, but she could hardly return it to the store after letting it soak in the lake. Nor could she take it to her brother's home. Hebron would never allow her to keep it after he had made such an issue of her owning it. So what now?

Hebron rarely came to the lake. If she kept the pole here, he would never know. The fallen log she normally sat on was hollow on one end. She knelt down to check and see if it would work as a storage locker. The rotted-out area was almost big enough to hold the rod. Looking around, she found a long pointed branch and worked at making the cavity bigger. After five minutes, she had an adequate space. If she stuffed a little grass into the hollow, she would have a perfect hiding spot.

Dusting off her hands, she sat back on her heels. Somehow, she had to thank the person who'd rescued her rod. Surely, he would return to check on his find. She quickly opened her tackle box and took out her journal. She tore off a sheet of paper. After searching through her lures, she found the blue and green rattle-trap she was looking for. It was a homemade lure, but she'd caught plenty of bass with it. She pondered what to say for a few minutes, then wrote a brief letter. She folded the paper over with the lure inside it and laid the note on the log. She put the same stone on top of it, took a step back and smiled.

At least one thing had improved in her life. She had her pole back. She jotted a few quick notes in her journal about the wind direction and the temperature, then she tied a spinner on her new rod and cast it out into the water. The lure landed exactly where she had aimed. A second later, she had a hard strike and she spent the next half hour happily catching and releasing fish. Her one regret was that the friendly fisherman wasn't here to enjoy the evening, too.

When she judged it to be about suppertime, she put her rod back inside the hollow tree and headed for home. During the long walk, thoughts about the kind fisherman who had given her back her pole kept going around and around in her mind.

Was it someone she knew? Joseph Shetler, perhaps, or his hired man? She thought his name was Carl King, but he wasn't Amish. There was speculation that he had been once but had left the faith.

Who else could her friend be? She couldn't tell from the brief note if he was *Englisch* or one of the Plain people. Maybe it was a woman. That didn't seem likely. The handwriting had been bold, strong and to the point.

Whoever it was, she hoped one day she would have the chance to thank him or her face to face.

Roman stepped off his parents' front porch into the cool evening air. The days were getting longer. It wouldn't be dark for another hour. Supper had been an awkward meal. His father didn't ask about his day. Roman wouldn't have known what to say if he did ask. Andrew had remained absent from the table. Roman didn't want his new working arrangement to put a strain on his relationship with his brother.

He went in search of Andrew and found him sweeping the sawmill floor. The boy was attacking the accumulated sawdust with a vengeance. "I should go get *Mamm*," Roman said. "She would be impressed. She's never seen you intent on getting this place so clean. It would do her heart good."

Andrew stopped sweeping but didn't look at Roman. "I'm not doing it to impress anyone."

"I know. I'm just trying to make conversation, but I'm not doing such a good job. This is awkward for me, too. I realize you're upset with me for taking the job in town."

He looked at the stacks of new two-by-fours sitting against the wall. They'd had a productive day without him. He'd made the right decision.

Andrew started sweeping again. "So how is your new job?"

"Complicated. *Daed* said he hired Faron Martin to work here. Do you think he'll work out?"

"It's too soon to tell. I guess he is all right, but it's not like working with you."

"Yeah, he has two good arms."

"But he doesn't know up from down about our business."

Roman chuckled. "I'm pretty sure the people at our uncle's office feel the same way about me."

"I don't believe that. You're twice as smart as they are."

Roman pulled a whisk broom from its hook on the wall and began cleaning wood chips off the counter near the doorway. "Thanks for the vote of confidence, but I'm like a babe in the woods. Everything is new. It's not like this place where I know every nook and cranny and every piece of equipment as well as I know the back of my hand."

"So come back." Andrew didn't look up, but Roman didn't need to see the tenuous hope in his eyes, he heard it in his voice.

"If only it were that simple, Andy."

"I miss having you around."

Roman stepped close to his brother and ruffled his hair. "I miss you, too."

"It's not the same. I've worked beside you since I was old enough to hold a handsaw."

"Andy. I've been meaning to thank you for your gift."

Andy stopped sweeping and looked up with a puzzled expression. "What gift?"

"Your fishing rod holder. It works pretty well."

"It does? You tried it out? When? Did you catch anything?"

"I tried it the other evening when you went fishing with your friends, and I did catch something."

"Wait a minute. You went fishing by yourself? Why didn't you come with me?"

"I wasn't eager to embarrass myself in front of others."

"I didn't think about that. I'm sorry."

"The fault lies with me, little brother, not with you. Anyway, I wanted to thank you."

Andrew brightened. "Hey, do you want to go fishing this evening? We caught some nice catfish below the bridge at the river."

"Sure, but let's go over to Woolly Joe's lake. I caught a new rod and reel there."

"What?"

"Honest. I pulled a brand new rod with an open-faced reel out of the water. It was a beauty."

"What did you do with it?"

"I left it there with a note in case the owner came back. I'm curious to see if someone claimed it, so I'm going over there now. Want to come with me?"

Andrew tossed his broom in the corner. "Sure. Can I get my rod? We've got time to get in a little fishing, don't we?"

Roman smiled at his excitement. "Get your rod and go get a sandwich from mother. I know you missed supper."

"Good idea. I'm starving." He took off toward the house at a run. He reappeared with a sandwich in one hand and a second one in a plastic bag sticking out of his pocket.

It was nearly dusk by the time Roman and Andrew reached the north end of the lakeshore. "Is this the place you left the pole?" Andrew asked.

"*Nee,* it's farther along on the east side."

Roman nearly missed the path, but he managed to locate the fallen log after a brief search.

Andrew turned around once in the small clearing. "I don't see it. Looks like somebody took it home."

"But they left my note." He picked up the piece of paper weighted down with a rock. Once he had it in his hand, he realized it was a larger sheet of paper than the one he'd left the other day. It had been folded in half. When he opened it, something fell out. It was a fishing lure in the shape of a small fish, a plug, obviously hand-carved and painted with iridescent blue and green colors.

He held the page to catch the fading light from the setting sun.

Dear Friendly Fisherman,
You have no idea how happy I was to see my new rod and reel resting against this log today. I knew when I read your note that a true sportsman had recovered my possession. At a time when everything seems to be going wrong in my life, you have created a bright spot with your kindness. As a small token of my thanks, I'm leaving this jig. It isn't much, but if you cast it along the rocky outcropping to the west, you should land a nice bass or two with it. Thank you again.
A Happy Angler

Roman grinned. He'd managed to make someone happy. He was glad that he'd left the fishing pole behind. The good Lord had used him to comfort a stranger.

"What's that?" Andrew asked.

"A note of thanks and a fishing lure for my trouble." The pole had done more than make a stranger happy. It had given Roman a reason to come to the lake with his brother. How strange to think a lost rod and reel was God's tool to mend the rift between them.

"That's cool. Why don't you give it a try?"

Roman hesitated. He didn't want to look like a fool in front of Andrew. He couldn't tie on the lure. Besides, what if he hooked a fish and couldn't reel it in? He almost said no, but something in his brother's eyes stopped him.

Instead, he said, "I believe I will if you rig it for me. I'm not very good at knots with one hand yet." It was the first time he had asked Andrew for any kind of help.

"Not a problem." Andrew grinned from ear to ear. He soon had the iridescent fish secured to the end of Roman's line. When he stepped back, Roman approached the shore and located the spot the thank-you note had mentioned. On his fourth cast, he felt a strike. "I've got one."

"Do you need me to help?" Andrew put his own pole down and moved to Roman's side.

"I think I can manage." It was hard to crank the reel one-handed with a fighting fish on the other end, but Roman realized he was enjoying the challenge.

"Lean back and keep your rod tip up. Giving him a little more line." Andrew continued to call out instructions until Roman landed the fish. At that point, he raced to the water to grab their prize.

Roman realized he was grinning from ear to ear now, too. If he could do this, he could do other things. He sat down on the log and laughed aloud. "Did you see that? I did it."

Even in the fading twilight, he could see Andrew's happy smile as he held the fish aloft. "You did it, all right. It's a beauty of a bigmouth bass. Must be four pounds if it's an ounce. If we catch a few more, *Mamm* can fry them up for supper tomorrow."

"I'm game if you are, but you know you're going to have to clean them all. I don't think I can manage that with one hand just yet."

Andrew's grin faded and then quickly returned. "That's a deal."

Later, when Andrew had walked a little farther along the shore, Roman took a moment to admire the colors of the sunset reflected perfectly on the still surface of the water. The sun rose and the sun set, no matter what troubled him. The world unfolded as God willed. Roman pulled the note from his pocket and read it again.

At a time when everything seems to be going wrong in my life, you have created a bright spot with your kindness.

He knew exactly how it felt to have everything going wrong. Yes, he had recovered the pole and left it here. It had been a simple thing to do, not really a kindness on his part, but he was glad that he had brightened someone's day in much the same way as the letter and the lure had brightened his.

The Happy Angler had more than repaid Roman's offhand kindness with a true gift. The lure was homemade. The maker had surely spent hours carving and painting the piece. Its value was much more than wood and paint. Using it had shown Roman he could ask for help without feeling helpless. He could do the things he used to do. He just had to learn to do them in a different way.

He turned the piece of paper over and wrote a note of his own on the back. Hopefully, the happy angler would return to the spot and learn that the small gift was greatly appreciated and it was so much more than a fishing lure. When he finished the note, he hesitated to sign it.

It was possible the happy angler was someone he knew. Like Roman, the anonymous writer wasn't looking for praise for what he'd done and had chosen not to sign his own name. Perhaps he had a reason for wanting to remain unknown. Roman decided to close the letter with the name the happy angler had given him.

"Andrew, did you save your sandwich bag?"

"*Ja,* mother likes to reuse them, you know."

"Do you think she'll mind if I keep it?"

"I doubt she'll notice. Why?"

"I'm going to write a note thanking this fellow for the plug. I thought I should put it in a plastic bag in case it rains."

"Good thinking. And tell him how well it worked."

Joann was on her way to town the next morning when Roman passed her in his buggy. He stopped the horse a few yards ahead of her and waited. When she came alongside, he said, "Good morning. I'm going your way."

It wasn't exactly a warm invitation. She thought she would have another two miles to mentally prepare herself to spend the day with him. That hadn't happened. She tried to find an excuse, but none came to her. Oh, well, she could hardly refuse a lift this morning without appearing rude.

"*Danki.*" She climbed into the passenger's side, and he set the horse in motion. She wished she had taken more time with her appearance that morning. She had picked her oldest work dress, determined not to think about what Roman Weaver thought of her. Now, she was sorry she hadn't chosen a newer dress. She felt dowdy and small next to him.

The silence stretched uncomfortably as the horse clipped along at a good pace. The steady hoofbeats and jingling harness supplied the only sounds. Joann racked her mind for something to say. She wasn't much good at small talk, especially with men. Finally, she said, "It's a nice morning."

"*Ja.*"

She waited, but he didn't say anything else. Apparently, he wasn't one for small talk, either. As he concentrated on his driving, Joann had a chance to study him.

He seemed more at ease today, although he glanced frequently in the rearview mirror that was mounted on his side of the buggy. He held the reins in one hand. He hadn't looped them over his neck as he had the first time she'd ridden with him. He was dressed as usual in dark pants with black suspenders over a short-sleeved pale blue shirt. It looked new. She couldn't help noticing that he had missed two buttons in the middle of his chest.

She didn't realize she had been staring until he said, "What?"

She jumped and looked straight ahead. "Nothing."

He glanced down and gave a low growl of annoyance. "I was trying to hurry."

He attempted to do up the buttons and hold the reins, but the horse veered to the left into the oncoming lane. He quickly guided the mare back to the proper side of the road.

Joann held out her hand. "I'll drive for you."

He hesitated, then finally handed over the lines. From the corner of her eye, she watched as he struggled with the buttons for several long seconds without success. Another low growl rumbled in his throat. "I'm as helpless as a toddling *kind*."

Roman didn't remind her of a child. Just the opposite. To her, he seemed powerful and sure of himself in spite of his injury. She'd never been more aware of being a woman. He gave up fumbling with his shirt with a sigh of exasperation.

She said, "Let me get them for you."

He took the reins from her and raised his chin as he half-turned toward her. Joann felt the heat in her face and knew she was blushing bright red. This was the kind of thing a wife did for a husband, not a casual acquaintance. Her fingers fumbled with the buttons much longer than she would've liked. When she had them closed at last, she jerked her hands away from his broad chest. "Got it," she said breathlessly.

"Danki." His gruff reply held little gratitude.

"You're welcome. Have your mother cut open the buttonholes a little more. It will make it easier to get the buttons through them."

"I don't need my mother to do it for me."

It was impossible for her to say the right thing to him. They rode the rest of the way in silence. Joann thought the ride would never end.

The awkwardness between them persisted throughout the morning. Joann tried to show him how to use the saddle binder but quickly realized it took two hands to position the pages and then remove them even though the actual staples were driven in by pressing a lever with her foot.

She pulled the pamphlet off the machine. "I'm sure Gerald can do any of the binding work that's needed."

Roman said, "I'll find a way to make it work."

"Of course." Determined to get past the awkward

moment, she said, "Over here we have the Addressograph and our address files. One set of cards is for the newspaper, the other is for our magazine."

"This looks like something a one-handed fellow can manage," he drawled.

Thankfully, she heard the jingle of the bell over the front door and went out to greet their customer. A middle-aged man in a fancy *Englisch* suit stood waiting at the counter with a briefcase in his hand. His black hair was swept back from his forehead. He wore a heavy gold ring on one hand.

"Good morning. How can we be of service?" she asked. He wasn't someone she recognized.

"I was told that Roman Weaver works here. I'd like a few words with him."

The man's serious tone sent a prickle of fear down her spine. "He's in the back. I'll get him."

She turned around, but Roman had followed her and was standing a few feet away. "I am Roman Weaver," he said.

"Good morning, sir. Your father told me that I might find you here. I'm Robert Nelson. I'm an attorney. I represent Brendan Smith. Is there somewhere we can talk privately?"

Otis had taken a carton of books to the bookstore next door. "We may use my uncle's office if this won't take long," Roman said.

"Not long at all," the *Englischer* assured him.

Joann had trouble stifling her curiosity as the two men went into the empty office.

Chapter Seven

Roman closed the door and turned to face the attorney representing the man responsible for the accident that had altered his life forever. He didn't invite him to sit down.

Mr. Nelson opened his briefcase on top of the desk. "As I'm sure you are aware, the trial for my client is under way. The jury has heard closing arguments, and we expect a verdict tomorrow or the next day."

"Your *Englisch* law is of no consequence to me. I follow God's laws."

"Yes, that's very admirable. I've heard the Amish offer forgiveness to those who have wronged them. Is that true?"

"I have forgiven Brendan Smith. I have already told your partner this."

The junior attorney had come to Roman's hospital room with a letter from Mr. Smith's insurance company. They offered money to pay Roman's hospital bill and repair his carriage. Roman rejected their offer.

"Yes, I was informed of the conversation. As you were told then, if you change your mind, the insurance company is still willing to make a settlement."

"That is not our way. It would not be right to profit from this misfortune. It was God's will."

Mr. Nelson smiled. "If everyone felt the same way, attorneys such as myself would soon be out of business."

"I am not responsible for how other people feel. Have you come to discuss something else? If not, I must get back to work."

"Actually, I have come for a different reason. It is possible the jury will find my client guilty of vehicular assault. If they do, it will mean jail time for Brendan. As you know, he has had several run-ins with the law, minor things."

"He deliberately destroyed Amish property. He and several of his friends beat an Amish man for no reason."

"Bad judgment, bad company and too much alcohol. He has paid for those crimes according to the law. Hitting your buggy was nothing but an accident. Pure and simple."

Roman wasn't so sure. He remained silent.

"My client also has a family. He has a wife and a small child. He has parents and a younger brother who depend on him. If the judge gives him the maximum allowable sentence, it will be a hardship for more than Brendan."

"I am sorry for his family. I will pray for them."

"I was hoping that you could do more than that. We, Brendan and I, would like to ask you to come to the sentencing hearing if he is found guilty. We're hoping for an acquittal, of course."

"I have no wish to become involved with your *Englisch* court."

"I can understand that, but if you come and speak on Brendan's behalf, ask for leniency for him, the judge might be persuaded to hand down a lighter sentence."

Roman remained silent as anger boiled inside him. He saw no reason to beg for mercy when Brendan had shown no remorse.

The attorney rushed on. "The Amish are well-known for their generous and forgiving nature. I'm asking you, I'm begging you, to speak on this young man's behalf. Enough grief has already been caused by what was a terrible accident. We'll be happy to reimburse you for any expenses involved. We realize you would have to hire a driver to take you to Millersburg, take time off from work, that sort of thing."

This man had no idea of the damage that had been done to Roman's life, yet he stood there offering to pay for his help. To buy forgiveness. In the *Englisch* world, money solved everything, but it couldn't give Roman back a useful arm.

"Is he sorry for the pain he caused? I have not heard him say so."

"I'm sure he is sorry, but we entered a plea of not guilty. You must shoulder some of the blame for the accident. You were parked in a poorly-lit location. You didn't have hazard lights out."

Bitterness swelled up inside Roman. He barely managed to keep his voice level. "I have said I have no wish to become involved with your *Englisch* court."

He turned around, jerked open the door and left the room.

Joann watched as Roman stormed out the front door. A few moments later, Mr. Nelson came out of the office. He stopped at the counter, opened his briefcase and held out a card. "Tell Mr. Weaver if he changes his mind he can contact me at the phone number on the back of this. It's my cell phone. He can reach me day or night."

Joann took the card. "I'll give him the message."

"I thought you Amish were a forgiving people. That's the way you're portrayed on television."

She didn't care for his snide tone. "We are commanded to forgive others as we have been forgiven."

"You might want to remind Mr. Weaver of that." Mr. Nelson snapped his briefcase closed and left.

Roman returned fifteen minutes later. He didn't say anything when she handed him the card. He simply tore it in two and threw it into the trash.

For Joann, the rest of the week passed with agonizing slowness. She constantly managed to irritate Roman while he seemed to delight in irritating her. It got to the point that even Gerald and Leonard noticed the friction.

Gerald approached her when Roman had gone out with his uncle to purchase supplies they were running low on. He stood in front of her as she sat at the front counter. "Joann, what's going on?"

"What do you mean?" She continued working.

"I've never known you to be so on edge. What's going on between you and Roman?"

"For some reason we rub each other the wrong way. I'll make more of an effort to be nice."

Leonard came in wiping his stained hands on an equally stained rag. He scowled at her. "Joann, my wife told me this morning that you're going back to the bookstore."

"I am."

"Why?" the two men asked at the same time.

Sighing, she propped her hands on the countertop. "Because that's the way Otis wants it."

Gerald crossed his arms over his chest. "We thought Roman was here as added help, not to replace you."

Leonard grunted his annoyance. "He doesn't know

enough to replace her. Although, he does know the generator inside and out."

She said, "He will learn what he needs to know. We just have to give him time. Please don't tell him that he's taken my job or hold it against him. I was here on a temporary basis, and now I'm going back to my old job."

"It ain't right," Leonard grumbled as he turned away.

Gerald gave her a sympathetic half-smile. "Well, that explains a lot. I know you like what you've been doing here. It's got to be hard giving it up."

"It is, but all good things must come to an end, right?"

"So they say." Gerald went back to his typesetting table.

Joann waited for Roman to return, determined to be kinder and more helpful. If only he didn't insist on calling her teacher in that snide way.

No matter what had been said between them, each evening when she went out the door, Roman was waiting in his buggy to drive her home. Each morning, he was waiting at the end of her lane to give her a lift into town. When Friday evening rolled around, he was there as usual. She was delighted to have a real excuse not to ride with him.

"I'm staying in town this evening. I'm having supper with Sarah and Levi Beachy."

Was that a look of disappointment in his eyes? It was gone before she could be sure. He said, "I reckon I will see you on Monday, then."

"Actually, I'm driving my cart in on Monday so you won't have to pick me up."

"I see."

He nodded toward her and then drove away, leaving

Joann feeling oddly bereft. She watched until his buggy rounded a bend in the road and vanished from sight.

At Sarah's home, Joann found her friend tending her garden. Long rows of green sprouts promised a bountiful harvest in the fall. Sarah was busy making sure the occasional weed that dared to sprout didn't stand a chance of growing to maturity.

"Why don't you put the boys to work doing that?" Joann called from the fence.

Sarah looked up from her work and leaned on her hoe. "Because I want my garden to flourish and not be chopped to pieces."

"Are you saying the twins can't tell a tomato plant from a dandelion?"

"I'm sure they can but it's safer if I do this myself. I'm so glad you could come for supper. Sally and Leah are coming, too."

"Wonderful." The women had all become close friends after Sarah's aborted attempt at playing matchmaker for Levi. The whole thing had been the brainchild of Grace, his sister. In spite of all the women Sarah had put in his path, he only had eyes for her.

Sarah chopped one last weed and then walked toward Joann. "How are you and Roman getting along?"

Joann sighed and shook her head. "Like oil and water. Like cats and dogs. Like salt and ice."

Sarah grinned. "In other words, just fine."

"Please, can we talk about something else?"

Sarah's grin faded. "Is it really that bad?"

"Every time I open my mouth, I manage to say something stupid."

"I always thought you would make a nice couple." Sarah carried her tools to a small shed at the side of the barn and hung them up.

Joann was sure she hadn't heard correctly. "You thought Roman and I would make a good couple? We barely knew each other. Why would you think that?"

From behind them a man's voice said, "It's just a feeling she gets. She can't explain it. It comes over her like a mist. She sees two people groping their way toward each other."

Sarah turned around and fisted her hands on her hips. "Do not make fun of my matchmaking skills, Levi Beachy. I found a wife for you, didn't I?"

He moved to stand close beside her. "If I remember right, I'm the one who found a husband for you," he said softly.

Joann chuckled. "If you two are gonna start kissing, I'm going to leave. However, I would like to point out that I knew before you did, Sarah, that Levi was in love with you. And I told you that, didn't I?"

Levi slipped his arms around his wife. "I remember all the effort she put into convincing me that she loved fishing. It was a ploy to get you and me together on a fishing trip, Joann. She hates fishing."

Sarah cupped his cheek with one hand. "I don't mind fishing. As long as I don't have to touch them, clean them or take them off the hook. If you wanted a fishing buddy instead of a wife you should've asked Joann to marry you."

Levi looked at Joann. "If I had only known, I would've given you much more serious consideration."

Joann giggled. "I'm afraid Sarah is the only one brave enough to take on you and the twins. I wouldn't have the heart for it."

"Speaking of the twins," Levi said as he looked around, "where are they?"

"They went to a singing party at David and Martha

Nissley's place." She whispered to Joann, "The Miller twins are going to be there."

Levi scowled. "Those girls are too young to be going out."

Sarah patted his arm. "They're old enough to catch our boys' attention. Get used to it, Levi. Once Grace is married, the boys will soon follow suit."

"Hey, that will leave us all alone, my love. Nice."

"Until the babies start arriving," Joann added with a chuckle.

Sarah took Levi's hand and began walking toward the house. "We should go in. I'm sure Grace has supper about ready."

He stopped in his tracks. "Grace is cooking supper?"

Sarah blew a strand of blond hair off her face. *"Ja."*

He turned to Joann. "If we hurry, we can beat the crowd to the Shoofly Pie Café."

Sarah yanked him toward the house. "Stop it. Grace's cooking has gotten much better."

He gave her a quick peck on the cheek. "She'll never make a peach pie better than yours, *liebchen.* Remember that, Joann. The way to a man's heart is through his stomach. Good looks fade, good cooking never does."

Joann followed her friends to the house. Finding a way to a man's heart wasn't an issue for her. Her looks were nothing special, so it wouldn't matter if they faded. Her last thought before she stepped into the house was to wonder what type of pie Roman liked best.

It wasn't until early Saturday morning that Joann had a chance to get away and go fishing again. She packed a couple of pieces of cold fried chicken left over from lunch, a few carrots and an apple along with a pint jar filled with lemonade into her quilted bag. She left a note for her brother and his family telling them she wouldn't be home for the noon meal. When she arrived at the hollow log, she wasn't surprised, but she was disappointed when there was no message waiting for her.

She left her pole in its hiding place. She didn't really feel like fishing. She just needed to be by herself. The day had been warm, so she slipped off her shoes, gathered up her skirt and waded knee-deep into the cold water.

The muck and moss squished between her toes. When she stood still, she could see tiny minnows swimming around her feet, eager to investigate the new intruder in their watery domain. She looked over the calm surface of the lake and blew out a deep breath. It was such a good place. She always felt happy when she was here.

A splash off to the left made her look that way. She didn't see the fish, but something white caught her attention. She waded toward a stand of cattails. Nestled among the reeds at the edge of the water was a plastic bag. She picked it up and recognized her letter tucked inside. With growing excitement, she opened the bag and pulled out her note. On the back, she saw her unknown friend had written another letter. Quickly, she waded back to shore and sat down to read it.

Dear Happy Angler,
I'm glad the pole has been returned to its rightful owner. Strange how things work out sometimes. You don't owe me any thanks, but I appreciate the lure. I caught two nice four-pounders with it in the spot you suggested. Your gift brought me much more than a pair of fish. It brought me closer to someone I care about. Thank you for that. Like you, little seems to be going right in

my life. I won't bore you with the details. I will say that something about this peaceful spot makes my troubles seem smaller. Perhaps it's only that I've gained some perspective while enjoying the quiet stillness of this lake. It's a good place to sit and refresh my soul. I hope it has refreshed yours. The sunset tonight leaves me in awe of the beauty God creates for us. It is a reminder for me that He is in charge and I am not. Sometimes, it is hard to accept that.

Have you caught anything good lately?

A Friendly Fisherman

Joann hugged the letter to her chest. How strange and yet how wonderful that this person had found the lake was a place to soothe away the problems of life. What problems did her unknown friend face? She wished she knew. She wished she could help.

Joann smoothed the letter on her lap as she considered what to do next. Her first impulse was to write a note to the Friendly Fisherman, but was that wise? Was she really going to start a correspondence with someone she knew nothing about? Her innate good sense said it would be foolish.

Yet something in the letter she held called to her. Someone else faced troubles and was still able to appreciate the beauty of the natural world.

She read the letter again. There was nothing to tell her if the author was Amish or *Englisch,* single or married. She strongly suspected it was a man. He'd signed it the Friendly Fisherman, not Fisherwoman. Joann had encountered few of her gender who enjoyed fishing as much as she did. And there was the rub.

The unknown writer probably assumed she was a man, too.

What would he think if he learned she was an Amish maiden? Would he laugh at the thought that she spent her free time making fishing lures and studying the lakes and ponds around Hope Springs? Would he even reply to her note if he knew the truth?

She wrestled with her conscience. It was wonderful to find someone who saw this place the way she saw it: as a God-given gift that refreshed her soul.

On the other hand, exchanging letters with a stranger would be frowned upon by her family. If he were *Englisch,* her brothers might forbid it outright. Joann realized she had started down a slippery slope. First, by hiding the pole her brother had tossed in the lake. Now, she was considering a secret correspondence, as well. The thought of doing something forbidden was romantic and exciting. When would something exciting come into her life again? Quite likely, never.

She read the letter for a third time. This fisherman, whoever he was, wasn't eager to be known. Otherwise, he would've signed his true name. He might be someone she knew who was troubled. Didn't she have an obligation to help in her own small way?

The smart thing to do would be to toss the note away and not write another one.

Joann, who had long accepted that she was a smart woman, chose the unwise course. She pulled out her journal and wrote another letter.

When she was finished, she read it over. Nothing hinted that she was a female. She'd taken pains to make her writing dark and bold. Nothing hinted that she was Amish, either, only that she had faith in the healing power of God's love. She hoped it would find its way into the Friendly Fisherman's possession and cheer him.

With that in mind, she drank the rest of her lemonade, then rinsed and dried the jar with a corner of her apron. She tore the page out of her journal, put the letter inside the jar and screwed on the lid. The log had a knothole in its side where a branch had broken off the tree long ago. The jar fit perfectly inside the cavity.

Would the Friendly Fisherman find it? It wasn't apparent to the casual observer and that was the way she wanted it. She gathered a handful of small pebbles from the shore and laid them on the ground in the shape of an arrow pointing to the knothole. It was a subtle clue, but if the other fisherman was looking for a reply, he would see it.

Joann ate the remains of her lunch and enjoyed a pleasant few hours watching a family of ducks paddle and dunk for food in the lake. Glancing at her note's hiding place one last time, she realized she couldn't do it. She couldn't continue the correspondence unless she was completely truthful. She didn't have to add her name, but her unknown friend deserved to know he was writing to a single, Amish woman. If he was a married man, his wife might take a dim view of their perfectly innocent letters. She took out her note and added a postscript. Then, she started for home with a new and profound sense of excitement bubbling through her. She'd come as often as she could to check her makeshift mailbox.

Perhaps she might even meet her Friendly Fisherman.

Chapter Eight

"What's the lesson for today, teacher?"

Joann kept her temper in check by praying for patience. It was finally Wednesday morning. Only two more days of his constant company. She could hardly wait.

Roman leaned on the counter in front of her with that annoying grin on his face. He knew she hated it when he called her teacher in that mocking tone. Oh yes, he knew, and he made a point of calling her that every day since he'd started.

"What's the matter, teacher? Has the cat got your tongue?"

She was determined to be pleasant in spite of his taunts. "We're going to the Walnut Valley school board meeting."

Walnut Valley was one of several Amish schools that dotted the county. Leah Belier was the teacher there. The school stood a few miles west of Hope Springs, on Pleasant View Road.

He grinned. "So my teacher is taking me to school."

"*Ja.* Be careful, or you'll learn something," she snapped as she walked out the door. He followed close behind her.

She had driven her pony and cart to work that day, so she wouldn't waste as much time getting to and from the school. She unhitched Barney and climbed into the cart. Roman climbed in beside her and reached for the reins. "I'll drive."

"I'm quite capable of driving my own cart to Walnut Valley without any assistance from you."

His hand closed over her wrist in a firm grip. "No point in taking two vehicles. I may only have the use of one arm, but I can handle a pony cart. I drive or we sit here all day."

"Okay." She quickly relinquished her hold and tried to rub away the tingling sensation his touch caused.

He frowned at her. "Did I hurt you?"

"*Nee,* I'm fine." She folded her arms tightly across her chest and scooted to the far edge of the seat. She'd never admit his touch did funny things to her insides. It wasn't that she liked him. It had to be something else.

Roman glanced at the woman seated beside him. She looked as jumpy as a cricket in a henhouse. Why was she so nervous? Surely, she wasn't afraid to be alone with him. Her tongue was sharp enough to fend off any man.

She noticed his gaze. "It would be nice if we weren't late," she said tartly.

No, she wasn't afraid. He backed the tawny-brown pony into the street and sent him trotting down the road. After traveling in silence for a mile, he asked, "What kind of things will you report from this meeting and others like it?"

She began to relax. "Not me. You'll be writing up this report. Did you get a notebook as I suggested? If not, I have one you can use."

"I brought a notebook and two pens, teacher. I'm prepared."

She bristled. "Basically, you should take note of things that are important to the community. People want to know if the school has enough funds for the coming year. They want to know who the new school board officials are and if there are any needs among the children."

"What kind of needs?"

"Well, last year one of the children starting in the first grade was in a wheelchair. The school needed to install ramps and make all areas of the school wheelchair accessible. Your uncle ran the story in his paper and a large number of people, including your father, showed up to help remodel the building."

"I remember the day. He took a load of wood with him to donate."

"Were you there?" she asked.

"I stayed to work in the sawmill, but my mother and brother went to help."

She fell silent for a while. He concentrated on driving. "I haven't asked what your father thinks of you working for Otis," she said.

"My father looks forward to the day I can return and work with him."

"So you see this job as a temporary one. I get it now."

"You get what?"

"Why you don't seem interested in learning the business."

"Maybe I don't seem interested because I don't have a good teacher."

That silenced her. She clamped her lips closed and looked off to her side of the road. He regretted the harsh remark almost instantly, but before he could apologize, a red sports car whizzed past as they were cresting a hill.

It narrowly missed an oncoming car and had to swerve back quickly in front of them. Roman closed his eyes.

He heard the crack of splintering wood a split second before the truck hit him. He heard squealing tires as he flew through the air. He landed with a sickening impact and tumbled along the asphalt. There was blood in his mouth. He couldn't get up.

"Roman, watch out!"

He opened his eyes to see the pony had swerved dangerously close to the edge of the deep ditch. He managed to bring the animal back into the roadway without upsetting them. As soon as he could, he pulled to a stop.

He drew a ragged breath. "I'm sorry."

Joann didn't make the snide remark he expected. "Are you all right?" she asked quietly instead.

It was too late to disguise how shaken he was. He wiped the cold sweat from his face with his sleeve. "I think so."

She took a deep breath and sat back. "Take your time. We can go when you're ready."

"I thought you didn't want to be late."

She didn't reply. He couldn't bring himself to look at her. He didn't want to see pity in her eyes. "I expect you'll insist on driving now."

"There's nothing wrong with your driving. Barney can get skittish when traffic is heavy."

The placid pony was standing with his head down and one hip cocked. He could have been asleep on his feet except his tail swished from side to side occasionally.

Roman had to smile. "I think you're maligning your horse's character to make me feel better."

"Do you feel better?" she asked softly.

"I'm getting there." His pounding pulse was settling to a normal rate.

"Then Barney is glad he could help. Does it happen often?"

Did he really want to talk about it? Something in her quiet acceptance of the situation made it possible. "*Nee,* and I'm thankful for that. The doctor calls them flashbacks. It feels as if I'm caught in the accident all over again."

"I never knew exactly what happened. Would it help to talk about it, or would that make it worse?"

"I don't know. I've never talked about it before."

"Maybe you should. It happened at night, didn't it?"

"It was dusk, but not full dark."

"Were you going someplace special?"

"I was coming home from seeing Esta." He clicked his tongue to get Barney moving.

"So you were alone when it happened."

"*Ja.*"

"I imagine you were thankful she wasn't with you."

"It wasn't a pretty sight, that's for sure." He stopped talking as he thought back to that evening. Some of it was a blur. Some of it was painfully clear.

"My horse had started limping. I thought that maybe he'd picked up a stone in his shoe. I pulled over to the side of the road and got out. It was a cold and windy winter evening. I left the door open. I don't know why I did that."

"Maybe to block the wind off you while you checked the horse."

"Maybe. I don't remember. The man said he didn't see me. He went around thinking he had left enough room. Only, he hit the door and then me. It happened so fast. One second I'm standing by the side of the road and the next second I'm lying face down, and I can't get up."

"It must have been terrible."

"I could taste blood in my mouth but couldn't get any

air into my lungs. I thought I was dying. We're supposed to think about God when we're dying. I didn't. I just wanted to get up and take a breath." He was ashamed of that. It was a betrayal of his faith. Why had he told her that?

She was quiet for a time, then she said, "You may not have been thinking about God, but He was thinking about you. We really are his children, you know. Children sometimes get frightened. That doesn't make them bad children. Our Father understands that."

She had managed to hit the nail on the head. He had been terrified of dying. The fear still lingered.

The sound of a siren startled them both. They turned to look behind them. The sheriff's cruiser, with red lights flashing, swept past them. He turned off the roadway a quarter of a mile ahead of them.

Joann stood to get a better look. "I think he's going to the school. I wonder what's wrong."

"Sit down and I'll get us there a little faster." He slapped the reins against the pony's rump. Barney responded with a burst of speed. Within a few minutes, they were turning into the schoolyard. A dozen buggies were already there. Men were clustered in a group at the side of the building. Some of the women and children were weeping openly. The smell of smoke lingered in the air from a charred hole in the side of the schoolhouse.

Joann looked frantically for Leah and was relieved to see her being comforted by Nettie Imhoff and Katie Sutter. Sheriff Nick Bradley stood talking to them, a notebook in his hand. Joann jumped down from the cart and raced toward them. "What has happened?"

Leah looked up. Her eyes were red and there were streaks of tears on her face. "Someone tried to burn down the school."

"Who would do such a thing?" Joann was shocked.

"We don't know, but we must pray for them, whoever they are," Nettie said. Everyone nodded in agreement.

"Tell me exactly what you saw when you arrived, Leah," the sheriff said.

She wiped her face on her sleeve, and then stretched her arm toward the building. "I came early to get ready for the school board meeting, and I found it like this. Someone had piled the school's books and papers against the building and set it on fire. All the children's artwork, all my grade books and papers, all gone." She broke down and started crying again.

Nettie enfolded her in a hug. "God was merciful. The rain last night must have put out the fire before the whole building went up."

"Have you noticed anything suspicious in the last few days or weeks?" Sheriff Bradley asked.

Leah shook her head. "Why would they burn our children's books?"

"I don't have anything but speculation at this point. Maybe it was a group of kids horsing around and things got out of hand. Maybe it was something more sinister. Not everyone loves the Amish." Nick Bradley had family members who were Amish. He understood the prejudices they sometimes faced.

"You think this was a hate crime?" Joann asked in disbelief.

"It's my job to find out." He walked to where the men were gathered at the front of the building.

Leah gave a shaky laugh. "I've been complaining that we need new schoolbooks. I hope no one thinks this was my way of getting them."

Joann managed a smile. "No one would possibly think that."

"At least we'll have time to get the damage repaired before school starts again in the fall."

Roman, along with Nettie's husband Eli Imhoff, the new school board president for the coming year, joined the women. "This is not how I expected to start my term," Eli said. "Do not worry, Leah. We'll have our school back together in no time. Roman, please tell Otis I'll be in to see him about ordering new textbooks."

Roman glanced back to where Sheriff Bradley was speaking to the men. "I'm surprised to see the sheriff involved in this."

"None of us sent for him," Leah said.

Eli stroked the whiskers on his chin. "I wonder how he knew about it."

The Amish rarely involved outsiders in their troubles. What happened in the community normally stayed in the community. Their ancestors had learned through years of persecution to be distrustful of outsiders. It was a lesson that had not been forgotten. "I'll see what I can find out," Joann said.

The sheriff had left the men and moved to examine the charred side of the school. He squatted on his heels and used his pen to move aside the remains of partially burned book covers and bindings. He lifted an aluminum can out of the ashes. Joann stopped beside him and withdrew her pen and notebook from her pocket. She flipped it open. "Sheriff, have there been other attacks on Amish property?"

The moment she asked the question, she remembered the letter they had received from an Amish farmer whose hay crop had been burned.

The sheriff stood and pushed his trooper's hat back with one finger. "Nothing that I've heard about."

He glanced toward the group of men clustered at

the far end of the school where Bishop Zook had just arrived. "You're more likely than I am to hear about something like this. The Amish don't usually call in the law. Makes my job harder sometimes, but I accept that your ways are your own."

"We appreciate that, Sheriff." Should she mention the letter? Like many of the notes they received, it hadn't included a name or return address.

"Could you run a reminder in the paper that people should report anything suspicious to the law? It's part of being a good neighbor to watch out for each other."

Perhaps the man would read the notice and contact the sheriff himself and she needn't say anything about it. "I'm sure Otis will agree to that. How did you know about today's incident?"

"I received an anonymous tip. It was a woman's voice. She said to hurry or someone was going to get hurt out here." He placed the can in a plastic bag.

"That sounds like a threat." She glanced around, reassured by the presence of only her Amish friends and their families.

"I thought so, too. I took it seriously."

Roman came to stand beside Joann. "Sheriff, the men want to know if they can start cleaning up."

"Tell them I need them to hold off until I have my crime scene people out to look this over. They should be finished by the end of the day. Have there been any problems in your local church group? Any disagreement between members?"

Joann spoke up quickly. "Our brethren would not do this no matter what kind of disagreements they were having."

Nick shrugged. "People are people. I won't rule out anyone. How are you doing, Roman?"

YOUR PARTICIPATION IS REQUESTED!

Dear Reader,

Since you are a lover of inspirational romance fiction – we would like to get to know you!

Inside you will find a short Reader's Survey. Sharing your answers with us will help our editorial staff understand who you are and what activities you enjoy.

To thank you for your participation, we would like to send you 2 books and 2 gifts – **ABSOLUTELY FREE!**

Enjoy your gifts with our appreciation,

Pam Powers

SEE INSIDE FOR READER'S SURVEY

For Your Inspirational Romance Reading Pleasure...

Get 2 FREE BOOKS that feature contemporary love stories that will lift your spirits and reinforce important lessons about life, faith and love.

We'll send you 2 books and 2 gifts
ABSOLUTELY FREE
just for completing our Reader's Survey!

YOUR READER'S SURVEY
"THANK YOU" FREE GIFTS INCLUDE:
▶ 2 Love Inspired® books
▶ 2 surprise gifts

PLEASE FILL IN THE CIRCLES COMPLETELY TO RESPOND

1) What type of fiction books do you enjoy reading? (Check all that apply)
○ Suspense ○ Inspirational Fiction ○ Modern-day Romances
○ Historical Romance ○ Humour ○ Mysteries

2) What attracted you most to the last fiction book you purchased on impulse?
○ The Title ○ The Cover ○ The Author ○ The Story

3) What is usually the greatest influencer when you <u>plan</u> to buy a book?
○ Advertising ○ Referral ○ Book Review

4) How often do you access the internet?
○ Daily ○ Weekly ○ Monthly ○ Rarely or never.

5) How many NEW paperback fiction novels have you purchased in the past 3 months?
○ 0 - 2 ○ 3 - 6 ○ 7 or more

YES! I have completed the Reader's Survey. Please send me the 2 FREE books and 2 FREE gifts (gifts are worth about $10) for which I qualify. I understand that I am under no obligation to purchase any books, as explained on the back of this card.

❑ I prefer the regular-print edition
105/305 IDL F5DN

❑ I prefer the larger-print edition
122/322 IDL F5DN

FIRST NAME _____ LAST NAME

ADDRESS

APT.# _____ CITY

STATE/PROV. _____ ZIP/POSTAL CODE

"Goot."

"Is the arm better?"

Roman looked at his sling. "Not much."

"I'm sorry to hear that. The jury found Brendan Smith guilty of vehicular assault yesterday. His attorney told me that he asked you to speak at the sentencing next month, but you declined."

A cold look came over Roman's face. His voice shook as he spoke. "I have forgiven him. It is your law that seeks to punish him. His fate is in God's hands."

Joann had never seen Roman so angry. "Who is Brendan Smith?"

"He's the young man who struck Roman with his pickup. His attorney was hoping that Roman would speak on Brendan's behalf, talk about Amish forgiveness and all that. He was hoping it might persuade the judge to go easy on Smith. He's facing jail time."

The sheriff rubbed a hand over his jaw as he looked at the scorched building. "Quite a coincidence that we have a fire at an Amish school the next night, isn't it?"

Joann glanced from Roman to the sheriff. "What are you saying?"

"That I'm not a big believer in coincidences." He touched the brim of his hat. "Take care, Roman, Miss Yoder. I'll be in touch."

As the sheriff walked away, Joann turned to Roman. "Why would you refuse such a request?"

"I don't want to talk about it." He stalked off, leaving her wondering just how much hurt and anger he still carried inside. Forgiveness was the only way to heal such sorrow.

Roman couldn't help wondering if this was somehow his fault. Was it retaliation by the friends of Brendan

Smith? If he had agreed to speak on Brendan's behalf, would the school have been spared? He was deeply troubled by the idea.

As the sheriff marked off the school with yellow tape, Eli Imhoff stood on the back of his wagon to address the crowd. Bishop Zook stood at his side along with several men who were also members of the school board. Eli said, "We will hold our meeting here. It will not take long."

The people moved to gather around them. The Bishop spoke first. "Let us give thanks to our heavenly father that no one was injured, and let us pray for those who tried to carry out this grievous deed. May God show them mercy and the error of their ways. Amen."

The crowd, standing with their heads bowed, muttered, "Amen."

"The first order of business is to clean up the building and assess what needs to be torn down and what can be repaired," Eli said. "The sheriff will let us know how soon we can do that. Once we know what needs to be done to make the school safe, we will set a date to start rebuilding."

"We can put an announcement in the paper," Joann said. "We will need it by Thursday morning in order to make Friday's edition."

Bishop Zook nodded. "That can be done. I will send notices to our neighboring churches so that they may make a plea for donations at this coming Sunday's preaching. Please spread the word about our need. And do not worry, Leah, the school will be as good as new come the first day of class in the fall."

Eli looked at Roman. "Please tell your uncle that I will be in to see him as soon as we know what books must be replaced."

They went on to discuss other issues. Roman took careful notes. This was a story everyone needed to know about.

On the drive home, Joann sat quietly beside him. Roman wasn't up to making small talk or teasing her. She seemed to feel the same way. About a half-mile out of town, she finally spoke. "Did you tell the sheriff about the letter we received?"

The fact that there had been two fires on Amish property had struck him as odd, too. "*Nee,* did you?"

"I was afraid to, but now I wonder if I was wrong."

"What's done is done. The school will be repaired."

"I know, but what if this happens again and we could have prevented it?"

"Romans 12:19, Dearly beloved, avenge not yourselves, but rather give place unto wrath: for it is written, Vengeance is mine; I will repay, saith the Lord."

"You're right. We must leave it in God's hands." She didn't say anything else, but he could see she was troubled.

Back at the office, he told Otis what had happened. Otis shook his head sadly. "We shall do what we can for the school. I would like to see your notes when you're finished with them. I will want to add something about this to our magazine this month."

Roman struggled through the afternoon to type up his notes for Otis to review. Typing with one hand was a laborious process that he was sure he would never master. Across the room, Joann made quick work of her notes and handed them to Otis before Roman had finished a single page.

She came and stood in front of Roman's desk. She reached for his notebook. "I can help."

He slapped his hand down on it to prevent her taking it.

Annoyance flashed across her face. "I was only offering to type your notes for you."

"I can do my own work."

"I can do it faster."

Like he needed to be reminded of that. "I must learn to do it myself. You won't always be around to help."

"That's for certain," she said cryptically. She left and went back to work at her desk. When it was time to leave, Roman was glad she had her cart to drive. He wasn't up for company.

He learned when he arrived home that evening that news of the fire had preceded him. When he entered his father's house, he found his father and brother seated at the kitchen table. Faron Martin sat with them.

Roman's mother stood by the sink dabbing the corner of her eye with her apron. "Who would do this terrible thing?"

"Only God knows," his father said with a sad shake of his head.

Andrew looked at Roman. "Is it true the sheriff questioned you?"

"He spoke to everyone who was there."

"Nick Bradley is a good man. He will get to the bottom of this," Marie Rose declared.

Roman poured himself a cup of coffee and took a seat at the table. "*Daed,* do you know of a fellow on Bent Tree Road that had his haystacks burned recently?"

"I heard something about it from Rueben Beachy just yesterday. Why?"

"Did the fella know who started the fire?"

Menlo shook his head. "If he did, he didn't mention it."

"It seems like an odd coincidence, don't you think?"

"*Ja,* it does. Andrew, Faron, I reckon we can get a few more board cuts before supper." Menlo set his coffee cup in the sink, put on his hat and walked out the door. Andrew followed him.

Faron said, "Roman, could I speak to you outside?"

"Sure." Now what? Was this about Esta? Roman took a last sip of his coffee and got to his feet even though this was a conversation he was sure he didn't want to have.

When the two men were out of earshot of the house, Faron said, "I reckon you should know that I've been stepping out with Esta."

So Joann had been telling the truth. "I heard something like that."

"I didn't mean to go behind your back while you were laid up. Esta said there's nothing serious between you. If that isn't the case, you should tell me now and I'll stop seeing her."

Roman was surprised by how little it hurt to know Esta didn't see him as a serious suitor. He'd been foolish to think she would find a one-armed man a good catch. "*Danki,* Faron, I reckon Esta is the one to decide that."

"All right then. Just wanted to set that straight. Didn't want any bad blood between us, what with my working for your dad and all." He held out his hand.

Roman shook it. "How's the job going?"

"It's the best work I could have asked for. Your father is a good teacher and a patient man, but I don't think your brother is very happy that he took me on."

"Andrew will get over it. Give him time."

"I hope that's true. What about you? How do you like working for your uncle?"

"It's not what I expected, but I'm starting to like

it." To his amazement, he realized his words were the truth. He was starting to enjoy the job. Reporting and sharing information with the Amish community was important if they were to stay connected and strong in their commitment to care for each other.

As Faron went to finish his work, Roman began walking down the lane thinking about Esta and Faron. Were they meant for each other? If so, who was the woman God had in mind for him? He couldn't think of anyone. Before long, his thoughts turned to Joann and her conflicting feelings about reporting another fire to the sheriff. He shared the same feelings. What was the right thing to do?

It was a fundamental part of his faith to live separate from the world. Yet, like Joann, he remained uncertain in his heart as to what he should do.

He didn't realize until he was at the fence to Woolly Joe's pasture that he had been headed toward the lake. Well, why not? It was a good place to ponder the rights and wrongs of life. Maybe the Happy Angler had written him another note.

Cheered by the thought, he made his way into the woods and down to the small clearing on the shore. To his disappointment, there wasn't a message on the log. He wondered if his last letter had been found. He wanted the Happy Angler to know his gift had been appreciated.

Roman sat down and stared out at the placid lake. High cliffs topped with lush trees made up the north shore. He caught sight of a lone doe walking along the rim briefly before vanishing into the trees. Barn swallows swooped across the surface of the water catching insects and taking drinks while zipping past the surface. Their agility was amazing.

"Little swallows you fly away but return each spring on the very same day."

With a start, he realized he'd just spoken the beginning of a poem. He took out his notebook and balanced it on the log. "Where do you go when you leave this home? What draws you afar, what makes you roam?"

While he was groping for his pen, his notebook fell off the log. The calm peacefulness that the evening brought his soul vanished. Frustration hit him like the kick of a mule. Would he ever learn to manage with just one arm?

Why him? Why had he been crippled? Because some foolish *Englischer* had one too many beers before getting behind the wheel of his truck? Where was the justice in that?

He looked to heaven and shouted, "Why me? What am I to learn from this?" The birds he'd been watching scattered.

He closed his eyes and listened, but only the croaking of frogs and the drone of insects answered him.

God wasn't speaking to him tonight. He'd just have to muddle on. He leaned down to pick up the notebook and noticed a row of pebbles on the ground. They had been laid in the shape of an arrow. It pointed toward the log. He stood and looked over the gray bark. There was a knothole in the side of the log he hadn't noticed before. Something shiny caught his eye.

He reached in and pulled out a glass canning jar. Inside, he saw a folded piece of notebook paper. He smiled, opened the jar and took out the note to read it.

Chapter Nine

Dear Friendly Fisherman,
If you are reading this, you have found my make-shift mailbox. The last letter you left had blown into the water. If you hadn't been wise enough to put it in a plastic bag, it would have been gone forever. I didn't want to risk losing one of your notes again, so I came up with this idea.

I'm humbled and happy that my small gift has been of value. You won't bore me if you'd like to talk about your troubles. I've been told that troubles shared are troubles halved. Here in this beautiful spot, they do seem less important. I'll share my story with you and hope you feel free to return the favor.

I had plans to buy a house of my own soon. It's been a longtime dream of mine, but recently I lost my job. I can't afford the house now. The new job I accepted doesn't pay as well. To top it off, I have to work with someone I don't much care for. He has made it plain that he doesn't care for me, either.

I'm determined to make the best of it, and I

hope I can one day call him a friend. Until that time, I shall come here often to refresh my soul and regain some perspective. If I can't do that, I can sit here and imagine tossing him headfirst into the cold water. What a scare that would give the poor fish.

I shouldn't complain about my circumstances. My troubles are small compared to some. After all, how bad can it be if I have time for fishing? They only seem big because I can't see beyond them.

There, I've unburdened myself to you. I expect your troubles are worse than mine and you're laughing at me. Actually, I do feel better for having shared them with you.

The sky is overcast this morning, but I can imagine the colors of the sunset you saw. Were there clouds in the west? Were they fiery gold and rose pink? From this spot, all the colors must have been reflected in the lake. Two sunsets for the price of one. That's a good bargain in anyone's book.

I didn't fish today. The wind was in the north. Another reminder that we are not in charge, God is. I hope the fishing is good for you. You might want to try an orange, bottom-bouncing hopper to tempt a big old walleye that lives in the deep part of the lake. I had him once, but he broke my line.

I must close now, I've run out of paper.

P.S. I must add that I'm a single woman. (I almost didn't.) I'll understand if you choose not to write again. Please know that I have enjoyed your letters, and thank you again for returning my pole.

Your Happy Amish Angler

A woman!

Roman certainly hadn't expected that. A single Amish woman, to boot. Who was she? Did he know her? Was she a grandmother or someone's little sister?

No, the note said she had planned to buy a house. That was an uncommon thing for an Amish maid. Single women past marrying age sometimes lived alone, but most often, they lived with family members the way Joann did. If they desired to live by themselves, their father or other male members of the family would see to it that they were given a suitable dwelling such as a *dawdy-haus* as he lived in. He didn't know of any woman who had purchased her own house. His letter-writing friend was one very unusual woman.

Oddly, it did feel as if she were a friend, as if she were offering kind advice and gently steering him toward a better path. What would she think of him if she knew who he was?

"She would probably think I'm a poor, pitiful excuse for a man," he muttered as a wave of self-pity hit him.

He glanced at the letter again. No, she'd likely toss him headfirst into the lake and tell him to quit feeling sorry for himself.

Roman folded the letter in half and tucked it in the pocket of his shirt. To own a house was a fine dream. It was a shame she had to give it up. It took a good person to make the best of a bad situation and work toward creating friendship where none existed. Roman knew a moment of shame for his treatment of Joann. He hadn't tried to make friends with her. He gained delight in teasing her, in making her snap back at him. It wasn't well done on his part.

Tomorrow, he would turn over a new leaf and be

kinder to her. She was only trying to do her job. It wasn't her fault that he was ill-suited to the work and found it so difficult.

Roman considered what he should do. Finally, he brought out his notepad and started a letter of his own. Before he realized it, the note was two pages long, and he felt better for having unburdened himself. The Happy Angler was right. A burden shared was a burden halved.

He sealed the letter inside the jar and returned it to the knothole in the log as the evening light faded. He headed for home determined to do better at the job his uncle had given him and treat everyone there with fairness. Including Joann Yoder.

When he reached the house, he saw his mother weeding in her garden. He opened the gate and joined her. Stooping, he pulled a dandelion that had sprouted among the peas.

His mother paused and leaned on her hoe with a heavy sigh. "*Danki,* Roman. I appreciate the help. I declare, these weeds grow faster every year. I can hardly keep up with them."

"I'll take over the weeding from you this summer. My town job leaves me with extra time on my hands."

"Oh, that's sweet of you, but I enjoy being out here. I like the smell of growing things. I feel closer to God in my garden. It would be a blessing if you could do it once in a while."

"Whenever you want, *Mamm.*"

"Where have you been?" She started hoeing again.

"Over to Woolly Joe's lake."

"Ach, that's a pretty place."

"*Mamm,* do you know any Amish women who like to fish?"

She laughed. "Goodness, I know plenty of women

who like to fish. Your grandmother loved to sit on the riverbank with a pole in the water. Sometimes, I think she didn't even put a worm on the hook, she just sat there and enjoyed the day. Why?"

"No reason. I heard a local Amish woman was trying to buy her own house but lost her job. Do you know who it was?"

His mother frowned as she concentrated. "*Nee,* I know of no one like that."

"Then I must have heard wrong." He took the hoe from his mother and set to work.

It seemed that the identity of his pen pal would remain a mystery. Maybe it was for the best this way. He hadn't revealed his name, either.

Joann stepped off her brother's front porch and scowled. She could see the end of the lane from the house. Roman wasn't waiting for her this morning. Now she was going to be late.

She'd grown accustomed to accepting a ride from him. She made a point of telling him when she would drive herself and she hadn't mentioned anything like that yesterday.

She didn't have enough time to walk all the way to town by nine o'clock. She started running. Oh, she could just see Roman standing behind the counter and glancing pointedly at the clock when she finally got there. He'd be happy to tell her she was late. She could hardly point out that it was his fault. Odious man.

She reached the road just as a horse and buggy came into view. She slowed to a walk. Roman pulled up beside her. "Sorry I'm late. I had trouble getting Meg hitched up. My brother normally does it for me, but he was sick in bed with a fever so I had to do it myself."

"That's okay. I hope he feels better soon." She was a little winded as she climbed in beside him.

"Why were you running?"

"I thought you'd decided not to come for me today. I didn't want to be late."

His brow darkened. "I'm sorry you thought I would deliberately make you late for work. That was never my intention."

Joann hugged her book bag to her chest and remained silent as he set off down the road. That was exactly what she had been thinking. Who was the odious one now?

She gathered her courage and said meekly, "I'm sorry for thinking poorly of you. Please forgive me."

"I reckon I've given you some cause."

"Still, I was in the wrong."

A smile twitched at the corner of his mouth. A touch of humor slipped into his voice. "I never expected to hear you say that."

She sat up straighter. "I can admit when I'm wrong. It just doesn't happen very often."

He chuckled, but then cleared his throat. "What's on our agenda for today?"

He hadn't called her "teacher" in that annoying tone. Perhaps her goal of eventual friendship was possible, after all.

"We'll be putting together the magazine. They need to be finished before five o'clock tomorrow night so we can get them to the post office."

"How many copies do we print?"

"Twelve hundred."

"Are you serious? We don't even have twelve hundred families in Hope Springs."

"The *Family Hour* goes all across the county to

Amish and Plain folk and even some *Englisch* subscribers."

"There's still so much I don't know."

"You're doing okay. It takes time to learn it all. On
Friday, we'll get out the newspaper as usual."

"That sounds like a lot of work for the week."

"I thought you found our work easy." Oh, why did
she have to say that? Just when things were getting better. She could have cheerfully bitten her tongue.

He glanced at her and then laughed. "I have seen
it is not as easy as I once thought. When I'm wrong, I
say so."

She managed a slight smile. "I don't imagine that
happens very often."

"More often than you might think, Joann Yoder.
More often than you might think." He grinned at her,
and she blushed with delight.

They rode the rest of the way into town in compan-
ionable silence. Joann's high hopes for a pleasant day
vanished when they turned the corner and saw an ambulance in front of the office with its red lights flashing.
Leonard and his wife, Mabel, were standing outside.
The front window had been broken.

Joann jumped out of the buggy before it rolled to a
stop. "Leonard, what happened?"

"Someone threw a brick through our window. Otis
was standing just inside. The brick hit him in the head.
He was knocked unconscious."

Leonard's wife Mabel said, "We called an ambulance right away."

Roman rushed past them and into the building. Joann
tried to follow him, but Mabel held her back. "There's
broken glass and blood everywhere, dear. He's being

taken care of. They said we should stay out of the way until the sheriff arrives."

A crowd was gathering around them. Leonard said, "Did anyone see who did this? Did the brick come from a car or from a buggy?"

Everyone shook his or her head. Mabel said, "It was early, businesses aren't open, there weren't many people on the street, but someone must have seen something."

Joann glanced over the crowd. No one stepped forward. The ambulance crew came out of the building with Otis on a stretcher. Roman came right behind them. As they put the stretcher in the back of the ambulance, Roman spoke to Leonard. "Will you drive me to my uncle's house to get his wife and take her to the hospital?" The nearest hospital was more than thirty miles away. Too far for a buggy.

"Of course."

Mabel said, "I'll go and get her. Leonard, you should stay and talk to the sheriff. You were inside when it happened. Roman, would you like to come with me?"

"*Ja,* I would. I should tell my mother what has happened."

Joann spoke up to reassure him. "I will take your buggy and let your mother know where Otis has been taken. Leonard, will you call Samuel Carter, the van driver, and see if he can take her to the hospital as well?"

Leonard pulled a cell phone from his pocket. His hand shook as he tried to dial the number. "I can't believe this. Otis is such a fine man. He wouldn't hurt a flea."

Mabel put her arms around him. "It's going to be all right."

Leonard wiped at his eyes. "He gave me a job when

everyone else said I was through. I don't know what I'll do if anything happens to him."

Roman laid a hand on Leonard's shoulder. "We will keep the paper and the magazine running just as he would want."

Leonard looked at him, his eyes bright with unshed tears. "You're right. Just as he would want. I'm sorry now that I wasn't nicer to you."

"We will start anew, you and me."

Gerald came jogging down the street as the ambulance was pulling away. "What's going on?"

Roman said, "My uncle was hurt when someone threw a brick through the window. They're taking him to the hospital now. The sheriff will be here soon. When he is done, I want you to get some plywood to board up the window. Mabel, we should go before my aunt hears about this from someone else."

She kissed her husband on the cheek and hurried toward her car with Roman at her side. Joann and Gerald ventured as far as the doorway and looked in. There was broken glass everywhere. In the center of the mess was a pool of blood. A bloody towel had been discarded on the counter.

"What is happening to our town?" Gerald asked sadly.

Joann understood his sense of loss. First the school and now this. Was it a coincidence that it had happened during Brendan Smith's trial or was something more sinister at work?

Joann said, "I must go and tell Roman's family what has happened. I'll be back as soon as I can."

Gerald shook his head. "Don't hurry. I doubt we'll get any work done today."

"We'll get it all done. We have a magazine to get

out and a business to run. That's the best thing we can do for Otis."

"It'll take twice as long without him."

"Then we must work twice as hard."

She made the trip out to Roman's home as quickly as she could. Poor Meg was covered with flecks of sweat and foam by the time they reached the mill.

Marie Rose and Menlo were grateful that she had brought the news and had thought to send for Samuel Carter. It wasn't long before his gray van pulled into the yard. The retired *Englischer* earned extra money as a taxi driver for his Amish friends.

Joann helped Marie Rose bundle together what they might need and saw them off. Andrew and Faron stood beside her as the dust from the vehicle settled. "I'll hitch up another horse for you, Joann. Meg is getting a little old to be making so many trips to town," Andrew said.

He led the mare away and returned a short time later with a piebald pony hitched to a two-wheeled cart. "This is Cricket. He'll get you there and back."

"*Danki,* Andrew. I'll take good care of him. I must let my family and Bishop Zook know what has happened."

"I'll see that the bishop knows," Faron said.

"*Danki,* that will save me many miles of travel," Joann said.

She stopped by her brother's farm. Salome was pushing Louise on the swing in the front yard. They ran to her as she stopped the pony by the front gate.

"*Aenti* Joann, did you get a new horse?" Louise asked as she petted the animal's nose.

"*Nee,* Cricket belongs to Andrew Weaver. He only loaned him to me. Where is your father?"

"He and Mama are weeding the corn patch behind the barn."

"Danki." She watched the two girls return to their play. What if it had been one of them injured by a thrown brick? Who might be next? She made up her mind. She would tell the sheriff what she knew. It was little enough, but someone had to try to put a stop to what was happening.

Joan hurried around the barn and met her brother and sister-in-law as they were heading in with their hoes over their shoulders. She quickly explained what had happened. They were both as shocked as she had been.

Hebron found his voice first. "You must stop working at that place."

She couldn't believe she'd heard him right. "Why?"

"It is too worldly for you. To have dealings with the *Englisch* law twice in one week tells me it is best you stay here and help on the farm."

"I'm sorry, Hebron. I gave my word to Otis Miller that I would do a good job for him. I intend to honor my promise. I will be very late tonight. Don't wait supper on me."

She turned on her heels and left them staring after her, though she knew she hadn't heard the last of Hebron's opinions on the subject.

By the time Joann got back to town, the sheriff had gone and Gerald was nailing a large piece of wood over the broken window. He took a pair of nails from his mouth and said, "Leonard's wife just called and said that Otis is in the emergency room at the hospital in Millersburg. He's still unconscious, but they say his condition is good."

"Praise God for that news. What did the sheriff have to say?"

"He took the brick, but he has little hope of finding

who did this unless someone comes forward to say that they saw the crime committed."

"Did he think this was related to the school fire?"

"If he does, he didn't say so." Gerald put the nails back in his mouth and finished hammering the one he had started into the woodwork.

Joann went inside. No one had started cleaning up, so she got a broom and a dustpan and began sweeping up shards of glass. She had most of it cleaned up, when someone came in the front door. Expecting Roman, she turned around quickly to ask about Otis, but it was a young *Englisch* woman. Joann said, "I'm sorry. We're closed for business today."

The woman shoved her hands in the front pockets of her jeans and hunched her shoulders. Her eyes swept around the room and focused on the blood Joann hadn't had a chance to wash off the floor.

"I heard that the old man who runs this place was hurt. Is that true?" the woman asked.

Joann dumped her dustpan full of glass into the trashcan. "*Ja,* they took him to the hospital in Millersburg."

The woman finally looked at her. "Is he going to be okay?"

"We don't know yet, but he is in God's hands, so we do not fear for him. Do you know Otis Miller? I can give his family a message if you want."

She started backing toward the door. "No, that's okay. I don't know him."

She turned around and ran into Roman who was just coming in. Her face turned ashen white. She bolted past Roman and out the door. Joann stepped to the unbroken window and watched her. She got into a red car parked halfway down the block and took off. Joann grabbed a piece of paper and wrote down the license plate number.

Roman came to stand beside her. "Who was that?"

"I don't know, but does that look like the car that almost ran us off the road on the way to school?"

"I didn't get a good look at the car."

She turned to face him. "She wanted to know if the old man who worked here had been hurt. She seemed upset when I told her what I knew. How is Otis?"

"Awake and worried sick that *Family Hour* and the paper won't go out on time. The doctor said they needed to run more tests. They're going to keep him for a few days."

"We can see that the magazine and paper get out on time. There's nothing wrong with the presses. I'm willing to stay late, and I'm sure everyone else is."

"*Danki,* that will mean a lot to my uncle. What did you write down?" He pointed to the notepad in her hand.

"I wrote down the license plate number of that woman's car."

"What do you intend to do with it?"

She gazed at his face trying to judge what his reaction would be if she admitted what she'd been thinking.

"You plan to give it to the sheriff, don't you?"

"I think the woman knew more about today's event than she let on," Joann said.

"Many in our church will tell you it's none of our business. We must forgive the transgressors. My uncle has said this from his hospital bed."

"I do forgive them. I just don't want anyone else to get hurt."

He held out his hand. "Give it to me."

Joann's shoulders slumped in defeat. She reluctantly handed it over without looking at him.

Roman stifled a twinge of pity and took the note from her. He didn't want her getting in to trouble with her family or with the church.

"What are you going to do with it?" Joann challenged Roman with a hard stare.

"That is my business. Forget the number, forget you ever wrote it down." He waited for the outburst he could see brewing behind her eyes.

Instead, she lowered her gaze. "I need to get the rest of this cleaned up."

"Is the sheriff on our mailing list for the *Family Hour* magazine?"

"*Nee,* but he gets our newspaper."

"Then I want the notice from the farmer whose hay was burned put in the magazine and not in the newspaper."

"I'll have Gerald reset the type."

"*Goot.*"

She started to turn away, but Roman caught her by the arm. "I want to thank you for letting my parents know about Otis. He was grateful to have his sister at his side."

"You don't owe me thanks. I would've done the same for anyone."

Her tone had a sting to it. Clearly, she was implying that he wouldn't. He didn't say anything else. It didn't matter what she thought of him. He would do what was best for all of them.

Once the office was cleaned, they set to work finishing the magazine layout and printing the twenty pages both front and back that would be bound into the final project. Joann was everywhere, running proofs, carrying paper, refilling the ink when Leonard hollered that it was low and pausing to speak to the steady stream of people who stopped in to inquire about Otis and offer help. By late afternoon, the hardware store owner was supervising the installation of a new window.

Roman tried his best to keep up with the flow. Otis normally ran the saddle binder, the machine that stapled the magazine pages together. Roman had already spent some time thinking about how he could operate it with one hand.

Joann had shown him how to use the machine on his first day of work. She laid the open pages across the bar with her right hand and pressed the stapler with her foot. The machine moved the papers into the proper position and inserted a pair of wire staples. She then removed the pages with her left hand and laid the finished product in a container, making the task seem almost effortless. It wasn't for him.

He found a leftover length of plywood to make a slide and positioned it against the end of the machine. He had seen that he didn't have to take the papers off the bar. He simply put the next set on the machine and when it moved the work into the proper position, it kicked the previous magazine off the bar, onto the slide and down into the box. He could bind the pages almost as fast as Otis and Joann had done. He was feeling quite pleased with his ingenuity.

Leonard, his arms loaded with boxes of paper, didn't see Roman's invention until he banged his shin on it. He muttered under his breath as he hobbled to a nearby chair.

He dropped the boxes and rubbed his leg with both hands. "Who put that dumb board in the way? Are you trying to cripple me?"

"*Nee,* one cripple at this company is enough," Roman said.

He added another set of pages to the binder and stomped on the foot pedal with extra force.

Joann came and picked up the boxes Leonard had dropped. "It's a clever idea, Roman, but you should have warned us you put it here. A few words would have spared our friend this pain," she said.

Leonard stood and took the boxes from Joann. Grudgingly, he said, "I'm sorry about the crippled remark."

"Forget it. We've got work to do," Roman said, then continued to bind sets as his embarrassment subsided. Joann's gaze clashed with his briefly before she walked away. She was right. He should have warned them, but he knew she was speaking about more than a bruised shin.

The license number was still in his pant pocket. Would turning it over to the law prevent another attack? He struggled with his conscience as he tried to decide the right thing to do.

Chapter Ten

Was he ever going to speak to her again?

Joann endured the rest of the day without a word from Roman. Mostly, she kept her head down and stayed out of his way. He knew she'd been talking about the license number when she made that comment about warning folks. She'd seen the look of annoyance that flashed across his face.

It seemed that every time she made a little progress with understanding him, they clashed over something else. She should just give up and accept that they would never get along.

It was almost eight-thirty in the evening before they stopped working, but when they closed the front door, stacks of the *Family Hour* had been printed, stapled and addressed. All that was left was to take them to the post office first thing in the morning.

The sun was setting by the time they gathered in front of the building. Cricket was still waiting patiently at the hitching rail. However, the two-wheeled cart Andrew had loaned Joann wasn't equipped for nighttime driving.

"Roman, I have an extra set of battery-operated flashing lights you can use to get you home," Gerald said.

"Danki," Roman went with Gerald to get them and the two men made short work of affixing them to the tailgate of the cart.

Leonard and Mabel stood with Joann. Mabel said, "We're going to run over to the hospital and see if Otis needs anything. Can we give you a lift home?"

The couple already had a sixty-mile round trip ahead of them after a long and tiring day. They didn't need to go out of their way to drop her off. "No, you go on. I'll be fine. See you in the morning and please send word if Otis is worse. Tell him we are all praying for him," Joann said.

Mabel kissed Joann's cheek. "We will."

After she and Leonard drove away, Joann stood on the sidewalk and watched Roman climb into the cart. She said, "Good night. I'll see you tomorrow."

"Get in." His first words in four hours.

"Nee, really, the walk will do me good."

He sighed heavily with frustration. "Get in. I'm not letting you walk home in the dark."

It wasn't exactly an invitation, but she really didn't want to walk after such a long day. She climbed up onto the small benchlike seat. The cart was much narrower than the normal buggy. She and Roman were pressed together from hip to knee. The high arms of the seat left no room for her to move away from him. The result was a long, dark and exquisitely uncomfortable ride. He didn't say a word, and she couldn't think of anything to say that wouldn't sound foolish.

When they finally reached her brother's lane, she jumped down. *"Danki,* I appreciate the ride. I'll be driving myself after this, so you won't have to pick me up. Good night."

She raced up the lane like she had a pack of wild dogs coming after her. When she stepped into her brother's kitchen, she realized she'd been right about one thing. Hebron had more to say on the subject of her job. He was waiting for her.

She endured an hour-long lecture about being content with the simple life their ancestors had envisioned. She knew that Hebron believed what he was saying. She also knew he had her best interests at heart. She accepted his admonishment quietly. When he was finished, she explained she would only be working as a cleaning woman at the office starting on Monday, and he was content with that.

The following morning, she arrived at the office just as Leonard and Gerald were carrying boxes of magazines out to Leonard's small pickup. He would take them to the post office as soon as it opened. The usually dour Leonard was smiling. "Otis is being released from the hospital in the afternoon."

"That's wonderful news." She glanced inside the building. "Where is Roman?"

"He's gone to the hospital to help his aunt get Otis home and settled, so he won't be in today. It's just the three of us."

That would make it another busy day if they were to get the paper out on time, but at least she wouldn't have to be on her tippy-toes around Roman all day. What a relief to have a day without him.

She thought that was what she wanted, but she found herself thinking about him constantly and wondering how he and Otis were getting along. As it turned out, he was on her mind as much when he was gone as he was when he was hovering beside her. No matter what, she couldn't escape him. In all the excitement she hadn't mentioned it was their last day together. Would he care?

On the drive home that evening, she passed the turnoff to the sawmill and was tempted to stop. Would he be there yet? What excuse would she give for showing up like this? She realized how foolish she was being and hurried on, determined to forget about Roman Weaver. Come Monday, she would be back at the bookshop in the afternoons, three days a week. She would clean on Saturday when the printing office was closed. Their paths weren't going to cross very often anymore, and that was a good thing.

That night, she dreamed about meeting the Friendly Fisherman, a kindly Amish man who looked like her grandfather with his long gray beard, who laughed with her and not at her, and who admired her keen mind. She awoke early with a bubbling mixture of hope and dread churning her stomach. The sun wasn't yet up when she slipped out of her brother's house and made her way to the lake.

Please, please, please let there be a letter from him.

As dawn broke, Joann entered her favorite spot and saw a raccoon washing his breakfast of clams on the rocky shore. She smiled. "Good morning, sir. Are you the Friendly Fisherman?"

The raccoon paused, his tiny hands grasping a cracked shell. He bared his teeth at her, then waddled away to eat in peace somewhere else. She called after him. "*Ja,* go away you old grump. I know a fellow just like you."

Annoyed with herself for letting thoughts of Roman spoil the glorious morning, she crossed the clearing to the log and pulled out her jar. There was a new letter inside. She sat down, unfolded the small pages and began to read the strong, bold writing with eager anticipation.

Dear Happy Angler,
Your idea for a mailbox is quite clever. I never

would have thought of it. Now I know I can look forward to your notes come fair weather or foul. I'm truly sorry to hear about your troubles. To own a house is a fine dream, and it must be a hard thing to give up. I pray your circumstances will change.

Don't ever think your concerns are small or unworthy. I thank you for sharing them with me. I'll do you the courtesy of returning the favor. I also work with someone who would benefit from a dunking in the lake. Stubborn, willful, hard to please, quick to call attention to my failings. I sometimes wonder if it wouldn't be better to leave my job, but alas, others are depending on me so I must stay.

You're trying to make the best of a bad situation and develop a friendship with your coworker. You put me to shame. I must confess I've done nothing to better our relationship at work. With your wise words in mind, I plan to change that. I will be kinder. I will listen more and judge less. If I make the effort, perhaps the tension between the two of us will lessen over time. It's worth a try.

You are right about the sunset. Its beautiful colors were reflected perfectly in the water. It was a remarkable sight. Explain to me why a north wind kept you from fishing. It certainly hasn't been cold. I used to fish a lot, but not as much in recent years. I remember now why I liked it so much when I was a boy. It's the peacefulness. Well, landing a big fish is fun, too, although I have trouble holding a rod these days.

I'll be sure to try the orange hopper. Any tips,

fishing or otherwise, will always be welcome from you.

As ever,

Your Friendly Fisherman

Joann laid the pages on her lap and stared out at the lake. A strong south wind was starting to blow, and it made the water gray and choppy. She should go over to the north shore and try fishing for bass along the rocky outcropping there. It was spawning season for them, but she didn't unpack her pole. Instead, she spent a long time thinking about the Friendly Fisherman's letter.

He found her advice sound and wise. That made her feel good. It took away some of the uneasiness she felt about continuing the correspondence.

How was it that a stranger understood her feelings and took her words to heart when so few others did?

She read the note again. So he didn't know the rhyme about the wind in the north. He surely had to be an *Englisch* fellow. Her Amish grandfather had taught her the saying years ago. She assumed everyone knew it.

Her conscience pricked her at the thought that he might be a married man. He hadn't said one way or the other. Although she knew her letters were harmless, not everyone would think so. If he were *Englisch,* she should give up writing to him.

She pushed the nagging doubts aside. She didn't know that for sure. He enjoyed her letters. He looked forward to hearing from her and she enjoyed hearing from him. There was nothing wrong with that. She wouldn't give it up. She had already given up so much.

She took out her pencil and notebook and started a new letter.

When she was finished, she tucked the jar back in

the knothole and headed for home, where she had a full day of farm work waiting for her.

Later, her family took Otis and his wife a basket of food. They stayed briefly to visit and to do whatever chores the pair needed help with. Hebron might disagree with Joann working at the paper, but he would never neglect a neighbor in need. Joann had half-hoped to see Roman there, but his mother told her he'd already gone home. Try as she might, Joann couldn't stifle her disappointment. It didn't make sense, but she missed seeing him even if they did sometimes clash.

Roman spent the day helping his father and brother stack lumber at the sawmill. His mother had stayed the night with Otis and his wife. She wouldn't be back until late afternoon. Her men were left alone to fend for themselves when it came to cooking, but they managed. His father knew how to make scrambled eggs and cook bacon. They had the same meal for breakfast and lunch.

Roman was pleased to see that Andrew and Faron were becoming friends. The two joked around and worked well together. He was glad for his brother. He knew Andrew missed his company.

It felt good to get back to physical labor, but he realized by early afternoon that he'd put too much stress on his arm. It began to ache and throb wildly. He was going to be in for a long, uncomfortable night.

When evening came, his mother returned and soon had a hot supper ready for them. After that, the family retired early, leaving Roman alone in his small house. The days were growing longer and it wasn't yet dark.

He was restless. His arm hurt. There was no point in trying to get to sleep early. He wondered if Happy Angler had left him a new letter. He couldn't believe how much he looked forward to hearing from her. Maybe it was because she didn't know about his disability. They were equals, simply two people who enjoyed the same pastime. Roman didn't feel inferior or pitied. He pictured her as an elderly aunt, someone who loved the outdoors and freely gave good advice. What was she like? Should he try to find out? Would her next letter tell him more?

Finally, he gave in to his curiosity and walked to the lake. He didn't bother taking a fishing pole.

When he reached the clearing, he was happy to find he had a new letter. He lowered himself to the grass and used the log as a backrest while he read the latest note from his friend by flashlight.

Dear Friendly Fisherman,
When I arrived at the lake this morning, I saw a raccoon in our spot. I asked him if he knew you, but he grumbled and waddled away without answering me. Make sure you screw the lid of the jar on tightly if you leave me a letter. Raccoons are curious by nature and enjoy the challenge of opening things.

I'm surprised you don't know the rhyme about fishing and the wind. I thought everyone knew it. This is how it goes.

Wind from the West, fish bite the best.

Wind from the East, fish bite the least.

Wind from the North, don't venture forth.

Wind from the South will blow bait in their mouth.

My grandfather taught it to me when I was little. He would only fish when the wind was in the west or in the south, and he always had good luck. I, on the other hand, have not had much success improving my relationship at work. Don't think me wise. I'm not. I have a terrible tendency to say the worst possible thing at the worst possible moment.

Did you ever wish for the ability to call back the words you've said the second they leave your mouth? I wish that every day. Often, I think it would be better if I couldn't talk at all.

Perhaps that's why I enjoy writing these letters. I can always erase the words before you see them if I make a blunder. I hope you are faring better than I am with your troublesome work partner.

I will limit my advice here to fishing in the future. I've had success with spinner baits and rubber worms on this lake. Both are good choices no matter what the weather and temperature. Another bait you may want to try is a jig-and-pig. The bass really seem to like them, even in the winter.

As always, your friend,

A Happy Angler

Roman chuckled at the idea of questioning a raccoon about his identity. His unknown friend had a good imagination and a good sense of humor. As he read the lines of the fishing rhyme, he vaguely recalled hearing them in the past. His father didn't enjoy fishing but Roman's grandfather had. Maybe he was the one who had recited the poem. He died when Roman was only six. He had very few memories of the man. Roman's grandmother had lived with them until she passed away at the age of ninety-two.

He pulled his small notebook and pencil from his pocket and started a new letter. It took him a long time to get the words just right.

When he finished his note, he tucked the jar securely

in the hollow space. He didn't mind the walk in the dark. There was a full moon to light his way and he didn't need to use his flashlight.

To his surprise, he did see a light on the far side of the lake. Was it his unknown friend? Or was Woolly Joe looking for a lost lamb? One day, Roman figured he was bound to meet his friend face-to-face, but he wasn't sure he wanted to. Discovering her identity would likely end their unusual friendship. And he didn't want it to end. He could put his feelings and fears into words on paper better than he could speak them aloud.

On Sunday morning, Roman joined his family in the buggy for the eight-mile drive to the preaching service. It was being held for the first time at the home of Jonathan Dressler, a rare convert to their Amish faith. Jonathan was a horse trainer who took in unwanted and abandoned horses for an equine rescue organization. He had lived among the Amish for several years now and had married Karen Imhoff, the eldest daughter of Eli Imhoff, the previous fall.

The church service lasted the usual three hours. The bishop and two other ministers took turns preaching about forgiveness and about suffering persecution for the sake of their faith. In between, the congregation sang hymns from the *Ausbund,* their sacred songbook.

From his place on the benches near the back of the barn, Roman could see Joann Yoder sitting between her cousin, Sally Yoder, and her friend, Grace Beachy, on the benches to his left. Esta Bowman sat two rows behind them. Several times, he caught Esta smiling at him. Was she tired of Faron already?

Roman was glad he had realized Esta wasn't the woman for him. He was happy he'd discovered that before things had gotten more serious between them.

He didn't find her sly smiles, overly sweet voice and flighty ways as attractive as he once did.

He glanced toward Joann. He hated to admit it, but he had her to thank for that. She might not have a sweet and attractive way about her, but she had a knack— a sometimes painful knack—of helping him see the truth. About himself and about others. He had come to respect that about her.

Perhaps it was time he told her that.

At the end of the service, Bishop Zook addressed the crowd once more. "We are taking up two special collections today. One is to help purchase supplies to rebuild and replace what was lost at our school. We will have a workday at the school next Saturday and all are invited to come.

"The second collection is for our annual road use and repair. Our *Englisch* neighbors pay for road maintenance through gasoline taxes, revenue from driver's licenses, and money collected through tolls. However, we use the roads and bridges the same as they do, only we don't have to put gasoline in our horses or pay for a license to drive them. Our horse's shoes damage the roads in ways their car tires don't, so we must pay our fair share to keep them in good order."

Roman flinched at the thought of paying for road repairs. Why should he help the *Englisch* pay for road upkeep? So they could drive even faster and collide with more buggies?

The bishop continued, "Driving on well-maintained roads is a privilege. It is not a right. I urge you to give what you can. Last year our Amish churches in this area raised over a quarter of a million dollars for the fund. That money was divided between the state, the county and the township in which we reside."

Bishop Zook paused and then grinned. "For that amount, you would think I could get the potholes filled on the road that runs past my farm, but I reckon I'll have to give a little more to get that done." A ripple of laughter passed around the room. Roman didn't join in.

When the congregation was dismissed, Roman went out with the intention of speaking to Joann as soon as he had the chance. If he made an effort to mend fences with her, he could tell his pen pal he was making progress in becoming a better man.

In spite of his best intentions, the chance never arrived. Everyone wanted to know about Otis and about what had actually happened. He retold the story many times. By the time he managed to get free, Joann was sitting with her friends and eating, so he went in with his brother and filled his plate. A half hour later, he went in search of her again, but couldn't find her.

He learned later that her sister-in-law had become sick and the family had gone home. He consoled himself with the fact that he would see her at work tomorrow morning.

That evening, he headed to the lake in hopes that there would be another letter for him. He was disappointed to find his own note still in the jar. On the walk home, he pondered why he cared so much about exchanging letters with a stranger. He realized it was because he could say whatever he pleased without the fear of appearing foolish or weak. He had troubles, but so did the Happy Angler. Together they had found a way to share their burdens and make them lighter. Should he suggest meeting in his next letter?

Perhaps not. If his unknown friend wanted to meet, wouldn't she have suggested it by now? Besides, it might be awkward if they found that they knew each other. They would surely stop leaving notes for each other if that were the case.

He found himself wondering why his pen pal hadn't signed her letters in the first place. Roman hadn't signed his first note because he didn't want to take credit for a simple kind deed. So what reason did the Happy Angler have to keep her identity secret? Was it as simple as Roman's reason? Or was there a darker motive behind the omission?

The thought troubled him until late in the night.

The following morning, he drove to work through the pouring rain and arrived mud-splattered and damp. His uncle was already there ahead of him along with Leonard and Gerald.

Roman said, "*Onkel,* should you be here? Didn't the doctor tell you to rest for a few days?"

"I'm sick of resting. I need to get back to work."

"Velda was driving you nuts, wasn't she?" Leonard said with a knowing wink.

Otis laughed then winced and put a hand to the bandage on his head. "*Ja,* she means well, but it was time to get out of the house. She can fuss over a body more than anyone I've ever met. Are the pillows too high? Would you like some tea? Shall I close the window? Do you need another pillow? Shall I open a window?"

"It's nice to have the love of a good woman," Gerald said.

Otis grinned. "I'm blessed and I know it, but even people who are in love irritate each other once in a while."

Roman glanced at the front door. "Speaking of irritating women, Joann isn't here yet. I wonder if something is wrong."

"She has gone back to her work at the bookshop. I'm not expecting her until noon today," Otis said.

"Are you serious?" Roman stared at Otis in stunned disbelief.

Otis nodded. "Perfectly serious. She has returned to her old position, but she'll do the cleaning here on Saturdays."

Leonard muttered under his breath, "We finally had someone who could do nearly everything in this office, and she goes back to shelving books and mopping floors. I don't think it's right but no one asked my opinion."

Roman wasn't sure what to think. Was this what she meant when she said she wouldn't always be around? Why hadn't she mentioned anything about it?

Otis scowled at Leonard. "Roman will soon master all of the tasks that Joann did."

Maybe he would and maybe he wouldn't. Her feet might be smaller than his, but she had left some mighty big shoes to fill. Was he the reason for her job change? Had she decided she couldn't work with him? It disturbed him to think that might be true. He hadn't been exactly friendly toward her.

"Now, let's get to work," Otis said. "We're going to be reprinting the schoolbooks this week, all of them, grades one through eight. I have the list here. Leonard, the plates are stored in the back of the bookshop."

Roman glanced at the clock. His uncle had said she'd be in after noon. Fine, he could wait a little longer. He had a lot to discuss with her when she came in.

Chapter Eleven

Would there be a letter waiting for her today? Oh, how she hoped there would be.

Joann left her brother's house an hour before she needed to leave for work. Instead of driving into town, she headed her pony and cart to the lake. It was raining steadily, but she didn't care. She had a sturdy umbrella.

She glanced out from under it at the leaden sky.

"Please, Lord, if I'm driving all this way in the rain, let there be a letter waiting for me today."

She needed something to cheer her, something to get her through the day.

Thoughts of Roman had occupied far too much of her time over the past several days. He needed to let go of the anger he carried, but she didn't know how to help him. She prayed for him and for herself. She wasn't angry about what had happened to the school and to Otis, only saddened by the harmful actions of others. She offered up her forgiveness for the people who had committed the crimes. That should have been enough, but it wasn't. She wanted to prevent other incidents.

She hadn't forgotten the license plate number she had written down. If she gave it to the *Englisch* sheriff, would it be because she was following God's will or her own? Was she harboring a desire to prevent other such attacks, or was she seeking revenge? She wasn't sure of her own motives.

Vengeance was the Lord's. It had no place in her heart. However, she was human enough to admit she wanted the person who had injured Otis to face worldly justice.

She put her worries aside as she stopped in front of the gate leading to Joseph Shetler's pasture. Before she got down from the cart, a figure loomed out of the rain in front of her.

The shepherd's hired man stood with his shoulders hunched against the weather and water dripping from the brim of his dark hat. "How can I help you?"

Was this the author of her letters? Her heart beat faster. She'd never met him, she'd only heard stories about his reclusive ways. Carl King was much younger than she had expected. "I was on my way to the lake to do a little fishing."

"In this weather?" His voice was deep and gravelly, and held a hint of distrust.

She gave him a nervous smile. "I reckon the fish are already wet, so they shouldn't mind."

"You've been coming here a lot."

"Is that a problem?" What would she do if he turned her away?

"I guess not." He swung open the gate. "Just make sure that you don't let the sheep out when you leave. Keep an eye out for an ewe and lamb. They're missing from our flock."

Relieved that he wasn't going to stop her, she said, "I'll do that. Please tell Joseph that Joann Yoder says hello."

"I know who you are."

He certainly wasn't a friendly fellow. She would be surprised if it turned out that he was her pen pal. "You're Carl King, aren't you?"

"Yes."

Slapping the reins against her pony, she sent him through the open gate. As Carl swung it closed behind her, she looked over her shoulder. "Have you noticed anyone else coming here a lot?"

"No."

He looked impatient to end their meeting. She was keeping him standing in the rain. "Did you happen to pull a rod and reel out of the lake recently while you were fishing?" If he were the Friendly Fisherman, would he admit it?

"Nope."

"*Danki*. Have a pleasant day." In a way, she was thankful that he wasn't the one, but it was odd that he hadn't seen anyone coming and going frequently. He lived in the shepherd's hut near the pasture gate.

"Is there another way in to the lake?" she asked as she turned around. Carl was already gone. He had vanished into the mist as silently as he had appeared.

Happily, she found a letter waiting for her when she arrived at the log. She sat down and eagerly began to read, taking care to keep it out of the rain.

Dear Happy Angler,
I'm surprised Mr. Raccoon didn't stay and speak to you. I'll tell him that he was rude. I'm sure he will have more to say to you the next time you meet.

Joann grinned. It seemed her pen pal shared her sense of humor.

As for my work-related troubles, they have doubled. It is amazing how cruel and heartless some people can be. It saddens and sickens me. More than ever, I find I need the peace this place brings me. I'm bound up in a struggle between what I know is right and what others think is right.

That was exactly the dilemma she faced. To do what she thought was right, or to do what others told her was right. They were so much alike, this unknown writer and she. It was as if they faced the same challenges. It surely had to be someone she knew. But *Englisch* or Amish?

I never thought I lacked moral courage, but I fear that I do. Forgiveness is an easy word to say, but it's hard to mean it deep in your heart. I say it, but I don't mean it. I don't know if I ever will and that frightens me.

As for our troublesome coworkers, I suggest a trade. You can take my headache for a week and I'll take yours. I hope you don't think I'm making fun of your troubles. I'm not. I'm just grumpy and aching today. I think we're in for a weather change.

Don't be too hard on yourself. We all say things we don't mean. As for your coworker. Look for his strengths instead of his weaknesses. I know you'll find them.

It was good advice. Roman was irritating and reluctant to take her advice, but he had to have his own strengths. She would look for them more diligently.

And when she couldn't find any, she would think more about chucking him headfirst into the lake.

Shame swept over her at her unkind thoughts. Somehow, even when Roman wasn't around, he brought out the worst in her. She continued reading.

I plan to invest in a few jig-and-pigs. Thanks for the tip. Truthfully, I haven't been fishing lately, but I'll let you know what I catch in the future.
A Friendly Fisherman.
P.S. Please don't judge me harshly.

How could she judge him harshly? It was clear he struggled as she did with doing the right thing. She wrote out a heartfelt reply.

She folded the finished letter, tucked it into the jar and placed it inside the fallen log. She wished she could speak to her unknown friend in person. Wouldn't it be wonderful to meet here and enjoy a day of fishing together. She considered adding a request to meet, but shyness stopped her. He might enjoy exchanging letters, but who would enjoy spending time with a plain, lonely old maid? She didn't want his eagerness to read her notes turning to pity for her. It was better this way. For now. If he would reveal his identity, she might find the courage to reveal hers.

The rain stopped as she climbed back into her cart and headed toward town. Today, she would look for a hidden strength in Roman. If she discovered a positive quality about him, perhaps he would be on her mind less often.

When she arrived in town, she turned down the alley at the side of the building where Otis had a small shed for his employees' horses. She settled her pony on the fresh straw someone had laid down that morning. She made sure he had a pail of water and an armful of hay to munch on.

She entered the back door of the bookstore. Mabel was busy dusting the bookshelves in the small store. She held out a second dust rag for Joann. "I thought I would get started cleaning. I haven't had a customer all morning, and I'm bored to tears."

Joann slipped on a large apron and tied it behind her. She took the rag from Mabel. "I never complain if someone wants to clean."

"There is enough dust for both of us. I started by the front windows. If you want to start with the back shelves, we'll meet in the middle. How does that sound?"

"It sounds like a *goot* plan. Have you heard how Otis is doing?"

"I think he's doing okay. Leonard popped over earlier to tell me Otis had come in to work."

Joann frowned. "I thought he had strict orders from Dr. Zook to rest this week."

"You know men. They ignore their doctor's orders and do what they want to do anyway. Then they complain like small children when they don't get better. I have half a mind to go over there and drag him home by the ear. He scared the life out of me when I saw him lying amid all that broken glass and blood."

Joann began dusting. She pulled out a handful of books, wiped down the shelf and replaced the volumes. "Have they found out who did it?"

Mabel stood on a step stool to wipe off the top of the bookcase. "Not that I've heard. I hope someone wasn't deliberately trying to hurt him. It does make me wonder since Roman is working here, too."

Joann paused in her work. "Why would that make a difference?"

"Because of the trial. Brendan Smith is known to dislike the Amish. He comes from a family that makes no bones about feeling the same way. It's sad, really. If they would just take the time to get to know their neighbors, I think they would feel differently."

"Is there a young woman in his family with white-blond hair, about my height, very pretty?"

"Not that I recall. Why?"

Joann dropped to her knees and began dusting the bottom shelves and books. "A young woman like that stopped in to ask about Otis that afternoon."

"A lot of people stopped in here to ask about Otis. I don't remember seeing anyone like that. The whole community was upset by what had happened. *Englisch* and Amish folks."

"It was probably just a coincidence, but I saw a car like the one she was in the morning of the school fire."

"Did you tell the sheriff?"

Joann shook her head. She had hoped to put her suspicions about the young woman to rest. All she had now was more questions.

"Joann, I don't mean to pry, but I was surprised when Otis told me that you wanted your job here at the bookstore back. I know you loved working in the printing office. Did it have anything to do with Roman Weaver coming to work there?"

It was the question she had been dreading. What should she say? The truth was always the best answer, but she didn't want to make it sound like Roman had forced her out. Otis had the right to hire anyone he wanted.

"It was time for a change." She finished dusting the bottom shelf and moved to the next bookcase.

"After only a few months?"

"I wasn't needed once Roman learned his way around. I'm happy doing this. It gives me more time to go fishing."

Mabel shook her head. "You and your fishing. I don't see how anyone can like touching slimy, smelly fish. Yuck."

Joann was saved from having to explain her fascination with the sport by the bell over the entrance. Mabel went to take care of her customer. Joann finished dusting, ran the vacuum sweeper over the carpet runners between the rows of shelves and mopped the uncarpeted areas of the floor. She was cleaning the two large windows facing the street when she saw Roman walk past. He caught sight of her at the same moment and stopped. To her dismay, he turned around to enter the shop.

Roman stood inside the entrance to the bookstore and watched Joann scrubbing the window so vigorously he was astounded that she hadn't worn a hole through it. She was deliberately ignoring him.

Mabel was helping another customer. "I'll be with you in a minute," she said.

He nodded and stepped over to the nearest bookshelves where he had a clear view of Joann. Was she still upset with him about the license plate number he'd taken from her? He'd been waiting all day to talk to her. Now that she was within sight, he suddenly didn't know why he'd been so keen on it. He rubbed a hand over his jaw and started browsing through the titles in front of him without really seeing them. He glanced her way several times, but she continued to work at cleaning the windows.

Finally, he spoke. "It must be on the outside."

She stopped scrubbing and glanced at him. "Were you talking to me?"

He replaced the book he held and picked up another. "You've been working on the same window pane for five minutes. If the spot hasn't come off by now, it must be on the outside."

She took a step back from the window. "You're right."

"What did you say?"

"I said you're right," she repeated in a louder voice.

He chuckled. "How hard was that to say?"

She rolled her eyes and picked up her supplies. "Laugh if you like, I have work to do."

He put the book away. "Otis told me you decided to come back to your old job. Why?"

"How is he today?"

She avoided his question by asking one of her own, he noticed. "He has a bad headache. I tried to get him to leave, but he insists on staying."

"Stubborn must run in your family," she said.

"Tell me, why does someone who loves research, reading and writing as much as you do, give it up to scrub floors?"

She glared at him, her green eyes snapping. "There's nothing wrong with cleaning floors. Cleanliness is next to godliness."

He held up his hand. "I didn't say there was anything wrong with it. I only wondered why you chose it over working on the magazine and newspaper."

She looked down at the floor. "It was time for a change."

"Are you sure it's not because I work there now?"

She still didn't look at him. "I accepted this job before you accepted yours."

He wasn't sure he believed her, but he decided to give her the benefit of the doubt. He picked up another book and pretended to read the back cover. "Otis wants me to write an article for next month's magazine."

"On what?"

Mabel came over to him. "Are you interested in child-rearing?"

He looked at the book in his hand and hastily returned it to the shelf. "I'm just browsing."

"That's fine. Let me know if I can be of assistance." Mabel walked back to the counter and sat down. He turned to find Joann smothering a grin.

He liked her smile. He liked the way it made her eyes sparkle. Her grin slowly faded. She looked down. "What are you writing an article about?"

"The law and our responsibilities."

"Because of what's been happening?"

"I assume that's why Otis chose the topic. Perhaps because of my accident, as well."

"It is a relevant topic."

"What is your opinion? Should an Amish person call or notify the police when they are the victim of a crime? Does that go against our teachings of nonresistance and nonviolence? The Bible says in Matthew 5:39, 'But I say unto you, That ye resist not evil: but whosoever shall smite thee on thy right cheek, turn to him the other also.'"

She folded her arms and nibbled at her lower lip. "If you're asking me what I want done about the license plate number I wrote down, I would like to give it to the sheriff."

"There is a larger question besides what you or I would *like* to do. It's about what we *should* do."

"You believe we should do nothing."

"I'm not sure."

"By doing nothing, aren't we leading weaker souls into temptation?"

"How so?"

"Might someone decide it's easier to rob an Amish home because he thinks that crime won't be reported? What is our responsibility to him?"

"You think we should take temptation out of his way."

"Yes, but how? By keeping our money out of sight and in a safe place, or by letting it be known his crime will be reported to the *Englisch* law? Paul urged Christians to give civil authorities their dues with regard to taxes, respect and honor."

The fire was back in her green eyes. Why had he ever thought she was homely? He said, "You've given me a lot to think about."

"I look forward to reading your article. Do you have your answer?"

"I think so. We should feel we can report a crime and answer police questions if we're asked, but we shouldn't seek revenge. We shouldn't file charges or seek damages from others. I think in this way we will remain true to the teachings of Christ."

"You have forgotten the most important thing."

"What's that?"

"We must forgive those who harm us."

Trust her to point out his failings. Why did he think she might understand his struggle? He took a step back. "I haven't forgotten. Enjoy your new job." He left the bookstore, slamming the door behind him.

He worked the rest of the afternoon on the article his uncle had assigned him. Three times he painstakingly typed out his thoughts and three times he tore the page out of the typewriter, wadded it up and tossed it toward the trash can. He left work that evening hoping something would occur to him out at the lake.

He was happy to discover a new letter waiting for him when he reached his now favorite spot. This time, he had taken his pole and hoped to get in a few hours of fishing before dark. He opened his note.

My Friend,
It seems we share the same sense of the absurd. Mr. Raccoon has not put in another appearance. Clearly, he is ashamed of his earlier behavior and is trying to avoid me.

I'm sorry your troubles at work are getting worse instead of better. I, too, am saddened by the cruel and senseless behavior I've seen lately. Are we perhaps talking about the same events in our community? I'm referring to the Amish schoolhouse fire and the injury of Otis Miller when someone threw a brick through the window of his business. These nameless individuals may think they are hurting the Amish, but they are only hurting themselves. I feel sorry for them.

As for your personal struggle, I urge you to do what you know is right. That is usually the truest course. If you can, seek the wisdom of men you admire and take their words to heart. Very few people have lived a life free of pain. Some may even have faced the same issue that is troubling you. We do not travel though this world alone.

Forgiveness is not easy. Some hurts are so deep

that we can see only despair and question why
God has chosen this for us. Forgiveness is God's
mighty gift to the giver. It heals the one who was
harmed. It can also heal those who have caused
harm if they acknowledge what they have done
and seek redemption.

I hope you continue to draw comfort from this
beautiful spot, and I hope you find my letters as
comforting as I find yours. I will heed your sage
advice and seek the strengths of the man who an-
noys me. If I don't find any, I'm willing to make
the trade. You name the time and place.

The hardware store in Hope Springs carries
a good selection of fishing tackle. You can find
several kinds of jig-n-pigs there.

May God bless you and keep you.
The Happy Angler

Reading one of the Happy Angler's letters always
made him feel better. He didn't have to struggle with
his doubts and problems alone. This letter made him
almost certain that the Happy Angler was an Amish
woman from his community.

She was someone who was familiar with the recent
crime spree. She was also someone who advocated forgiveness even as she acknowledged how difficult that
could be. Roman's curiosity continued to grow about
the identity of his friend. Who could she be? He thought
of some of the kindhearted single women in his church
district. There was Sally Yoder, Grace Beachy and a
whole slew of girls his brother's age. Then there was
Lea Belier, the teacher. She would have free time to fish
now that school was out for the summer, but who would

annoy her at her job? Was she working somewhere else over the summer?

If he started asking his mother questions about the local single maids, she would start harping about grand-children again. He would simply have to wonder and hope his unknown friend would one day reveal her iden-tity.

Of course, it could be Joann Yoder.

That thought made him flinch. He couldn't see her starting up a correspondence with a stranger. Sure, Leonard was sometimes difficult to work with, but Joann had taken another job. Nothing in this letter in-dicated the author planned to change where she worked.

He mulled over the advice he'd been given. His friend was a very wise person, indeed. Roman spent the next hour fishing without much success. He caught only three small fish and tossed them all back. As the sun began to set, he wrote:

Dear Happy Angler,
You are so right. We do not travel through this world alone. You are proof of that. Yes, I was talking about the Amish schoolhouse fire and the brick-throwing incident. What will it take to re-store peace in our community?

As for forgiveness, I'm working on that. You write with great conviction about the grace for-giveness brings us. I think you are right.

God bless you and keep writing. I do find com-fort in your words.
Your Friendly Fisherman

He tucked the brief letter in their makeshift mailbox. He was starting to care a great deal about the woman who wrote such comforting words. Someday, he would tell her in person about the peace her words brought him.

That evening after supper, he waited for a chance to speak to his father alone. His father was a wise man. If anyone could help him with his dilemma, he could.

He followed his dad into the living room. "*Daed,* can I ask you a question?"

His father settled himself in his favorite chair. "Of course."

"I think I know who is behind the attack on Otis and the fire at the school."

"Who?"

"It's a member of Brendan Smith's family. I don't know what to do with the information."

Menlo stroked his beard. "You are considering giving it to the police?"

"*Ja.* I fear others may be attacked."

"I understand your fears. We must trust that God will keep us from harm."

"I know, but is that enough?"

Menlo was silent for long time. Roman waited for his answer. Finally, Menlo spoke. "If I see a house on fire, I will pray for everyone's safety, but I will sound the alarm and try to save what I can, be it my neighbor or his goods, and I will work to keep the fire from spreading. *Gott* put me where I could see the flames and help. You must pray for guidance and ask yourself if *Gott* has put you where you can see the flames."

"*Danki,* Papa. I will do that."

The following morning when Roman arrived at the office, he learned Otis wouldn't be in. Leonard was waiting for him with a note from his aunt. As he read it, Gerald came in.

"What's up?" Gerald looked from Leonard to Roman.

"Otis's headache has gotten worse. My aunt is taking him back to the hospital at the urging of Dr. Zook. She says that Otis wants me to take charge of the business until he returns."

Roman rubbed the back of his neck. The job was beyond him. Without Otis here, he really needed someone who knew what they were doing. Leonard and Otis were both waiting for him to say something. "How are we coming on the schoolbooks?"

"I printed twenty copies of all the first-grade books yesterday," Leonard said.

"I will get the covers on and get them bound today," Gerald said, then looked as if he wanted to say something else.

"What?" Roman asked.

Gerald and Leonard shared a speaking glance. "Otis wanted all the books done by this weekend," Gerald said. "I don't think we can do it. Not in addition to getting the paper out and finishing all the other orders we have."

"What do you suggest?" Roman wasn't above asking for help.

"Get Joann in here," Leonard stated. "She knows what needs to get done and how to do it."

Roman nodded. "Okay, I will ask her to help us."

"You will?" Gerald asked in surprise. "I didn't think the two of you got along."

Roman scowled at him. "I won't let my uncle's business suffer because of my personal feelings for the woman. Leonard, get started on the second-grade books today. Are there any that we don't have plates for?"

Leonard shook his head. "We have plates for everything that Leah has been using. It's a good thing too, otherwise it would cost more and take more time to set all that type."

"Guess we should get busy," Gerald said. "I sure hope Joann agrees to help."

As the men went to work, Roman sat down at his desk and noticed a note with his name on it. He unfolded the wrinkled paper and saw it was his first attempt at writing his article on law and order. There was a note in the margin. "This one is the best. Use it."

There was no signature, but he knew the note had come from Joann. She must have come in to straighten up after he left and found his discarded attempts to write his article, then salvaged one.

He read through the rough draft again. She was right. This version said what he wanted to say without sounding judgmental and without preaching. He put a new piece of paper in his typewriter and finished the article. When he was done, he felt a keen sense of accomplishment that he'd rarely known.

He opened his desk drawer and pulled out the license plate number that Joann had written down. Had God put him and Joann here so that they might see the flames of this evil and sound the alarm?

Roman prayed he was doing the right thing. He stapled the license number inside a copy of the *Family Hour* magazine and addressed it to Sheriff Bradley, then put it in the mailbox.

He drew a deep breath. Now, he needed to convince Joann to come back to work for him. He wasn't at all certain that she would.

Chapter Twelve

She was late.

Joann stabled her pony without giving him his hay or grain. He whinnied in protest as she closed the stall door. "I'll be back later to feed you. I promise."

It was only the second day of her part-time job and she was thirty minutes late. Otis would not be happy with her.

She should have waited to go to the lake until after work, but she had been eager to check for another letter and to her delight, there had been one waiting for her. She had lost track of time while writing an answer and now she was late. The letter was tucked in her pocket and the words came back to her now.

Dear Happy Angler,
You are so right. We do not travel through this world alone. You are proof of that.

Her words brought him comfort. She smiled at the thought as she rushed in through the back door of the bookstore and jerked open the supply room door. She grabbed her cleaning supplies and a broom from the corner, spun around and ran into Roman. The handle of her broom smacked the side of his head. She stood speechless with surprise and remorse.

He rubbed his temple. "Come into my uncle's office. I need to talk to you."

That didn't sound good. "I really am sorry. It was an accident."

"I'm just glad it wasn't a brick."

"Let me put this stuff back and I'll be right there." At least he hadn't asked why she was late.

She replaced her cleaning supplies and followed him to the office next door. Otis wasn't in. Roman sat behind his uncle's desk. His grave expression set off alarm bells in her head. "Where is your uncle?"

"He is back in the hospital. Apparently, there was some slow bleeding in his brain. My aunt called the bookstore and told Mabel they are taking him into surgery."

"Oh, no!" Joann sank onto a nearby chair. "What can I do to help?"

"I was hoping you would ask that. Can you come back to work in your old position? I don't know what your pay was, but I will match it."

"Of course. Just tell me what you need me to do."

"My uncle has left me in charge, but I am woefully unprepared to run this business."

He wasn't just being modest, he was worried. She could see it in his eyes. "I will do whatever I can to help. What projects are being run this week, and where do they stand?"

"All the schoolbooks are being reprinted," Roman began. "Otis wanted all of them done by Saturday. We have the first-grade books printed. Gerald is running them through the binder now. Leonard has started on the second-grade books. Fortunately, we have plates for all of them through the eighth grade. If worse comes to worst, we can delay delivery for a few weeks since the children aren't in school. Besides the newspaper, we have two hundred and fifty wedding invitations that need to be done by tomorrow, fifty new menus for the Shoofly Pie Café that were promised for Thursday and a half dozen miscellaneous business announcements."

"In other words, a lot."

A smile tugged at the corner of his mouth. "*Ja,* teacher, we have a lot to do."

She didn't mind her nickname this time. He wasn't being sarcastic. This Roman Weaver, a man determined to do the best for someone else, was a man she could like.

She rose to her feet. "I'll start setting the type for the wedding invitations. We can use the proof press to run them since there aren't very many. If you start on the layout for the newspaper, we should be able to get it out on time."

"*Danki,* Joann. For agreeing to help, and for commenting on my magazine article. I couldn't see the forest for the trees when I wrote it."

She felt herself blushing. She wasn't used to him being nice. "That is often the case with writers. That's why it's helpful to have someone read your stuff."

"I'll remember that."

"Once Otis gets back, I'm sure he'll proofread your work."

Roman's eyes darkened with worry. "I wish we could hear how he is doing."

She longed to ease his burdens. "We can manage without you for a few hours if you want go to the hospital."

He gave her a halfhearted smile. "I'm sure you could manage without me for a lot longer than a few hours, but I feel I have to stay here. This business is important to my uncle. Mabel will let us know something as soon as she hears."

Joann studied him in a new light. Her Friendly Fisherman had suggested that she look for Roman's strengths. She had found them in his writing and even more so in his love for his uncle. She looked forward to telling her friend how well his suggestion had worked.

They received good news about Otis an hour later. His surgery had gone well. He was in intensive care, but he was expected to make a full recovery. The tension in the office lightened perceptibly after that.

When they closed up for the evening, they had made significant inroads into their workload. Leonard was ready to start printing the seventh-grade books, and Joann had finished the wedding announcements. They walked together out the back door to where the horses were stabled. Joann had managed to get away long enough to feed her pony. He seemed eager to be on his way home. She was surprised to realize she wasn't eager to leave. She was enjoying Roman's company.

"Since you're working with us again, why don't I pick you up tomorrow?" Roman said as he headed for his horse's stall.

She frowned as she considered how she could make time to get to the lake now. She couldn't. Her letters would have to wait until things settled back to normal.

Roman led his mare out of the stall. "If you don't want to, that's fine."

"No, I want to, I mean, that's fine and it's nice of you to offer."

"But what?"

She smiled to reassure him. "Never mind. It's something I had planned to do in the mornings since I wasn't working, but it can wait. The usual time?"

He nodded. "*Ja,* the usual time."

She looked forward to spending time in his company more than she cared to admit.

The various jobs at the office kept them busy for the rest of the week, but it gave them something to talk about on their way to and from work. Roman remained approachable and interested in what she had to say. At least it seemed that way.

On Friday, Joann found him in Otis's office, seated behind his uncle's desk. He didn't look comfortable there. She couldn't blame him. His uncle's illness had forced him into a position he wasn't ready for.

He looked up. "Did you need something?"

"Do you have a minute to talk about the schoolbooks we're reprinting?"

He frowned at the paper he held. "Do we really need sixteen reams of copy paper this month?"

"That sounds about right."

"Okay." He jotted a note and closed the order book. "What was it you wanted to discuss?"

She took a step inside the office. "There are some changes that need to be made in the booklet on learning to drive a horse and buggy safely."

"I read through the book. I didn't see anything that needed changing. Besides, we have the plates for that one. It will cost more if we make changes and we've already agreed on a price with Eli Imhoff for the project."

"I wish you would read through it again."

"I don't have time," he said with exasperation.

"You, of all people, know how important it is to share the road properly."

He scowled at her. "I *was* sharing the road properly until Brendan Smith decided to knock the open door off my buggy with his truck. Either he didn't know or he didn't care that I was standing on the other side of that door."

"There's no denying you suffered a bad experience."

"Thank you, but that doesn't help me move my fingers."

"All I'm asking is for you to take a look at the booklet again, with your own experience in mind, and see if you don't think we can make it better."

"You will nag me until you get your way, won't you?"

She pressed her lips into a tight line. "I would hardly call it nagging."

"Is there anything else?"

"That's all I wanted."

"Fine. Now, I've got work to do."

"And I'll be out here taking a nap," she muttered as she turned away. How could he charm her one day and irritate her so much the next?

Roman heard Joann's remark, but he didn't respond to it. He had far too much on his mind. His uncle's health wasn't improving as rapidly as his doctor had hoped. Roman didn't have time to reread each schoolbook and make sure they were accurate. They had been good enough in the past. They would be good enough now.

Only, Joann had planted the seed of doubt in his mind. He couldn't dismiss it. He opened a copy of *Learning to Drive a Horse and Buggy* and started reading. Bishop Zook's words came back to him. Driving on well-maintained roads was a privilege, it wasn't a right. The Amish had to share the responsibility for the roadway upkeep and safety, too. Nothing in the text-book addressed this fundamental piece of information.

He, like many Amish, was guilty of being proud that he shunned cars and drove a buggy. Didn't he expect cars to travel at his pace and pass him safely no matter how long he slowed their progress?

The *Englisch* did not intend to slow down to the Amish pace of life. The Amish had to take as much, or even more, responsibility for safety on the roads. It annoyed him that Joann was the one to point it out.

His conscience pricked him as an overlooked truth wormed its way into his thoughts. It wasn't so much that she was annoying. What he found annoying was that she was so often right.

Later that afternoon, he stopped beside her desk. "Rewrite the section that you think needs to be changed, and I'll look it over."

Her eyes grew round. "Really? We're going to change it?"

"You were right, it needs to be updated."

"Oh, that was hard for you to say, wasn't it?"

He struggled to hide a smile. "You have no idea."

"I'm glad you took this job. It suits you."

"Are you going to the school benefit on Saturday?" he asked.

"*Ja,* I planned on it."

"Do you want to help me take the books out there?"

She hesitated, then nodded. "Sure. Shall I meet you here?"

"I'll pick you up at the usual time."

"Can we make it an hour later?" she asked hopefully. "I have something I'd like to do first."

"I don't see why not."

"Great." She smiled brightly and his mood lightened.

He found he was reluctant to walk away. "My mother wants to come with me. *Daed* and Andrew will be along later with the lumber that's needed."

"That will be fine."

He still didn't move.

She raised one eyebrow. "Is there something else?"

He cleared his throat. "*Nee,* I'll let you get back to your nap."

"*Danki.*" She swooped the paperwork on her desk into one large pile and laid her head on it.

He chuckled as he went back to his uncle's office. He had no idea she had such a cute sense of humor. There was more to her than he once suspected.

In spite of the heavy workload, they were able to get everything finished on time.

Roman's good mood lasted until Saturday morning. His mother was bustling around getting food, plates and glasses ready to help feed the people who would be working at the school that day.

She handed him a picnic basket to put in his buggy and said, "Esta Barkman asked if she could ride along with us. I told her we'd pick her up. I hope that's okay."

Esta and Joann in the same buggy. That should make for an interesting ride to the school. His mother was humming as she worked. That wasn't like her.

He suddenly had a bad feeling about the day.

Joann hurried toward the lake early on Saturday morning. She hadn't had a chance to check for a new letter since she had resumed her old job. It had only been a few days, but it seemed much too long.

When she reached the log, she was disappointed when she saw her letter was still in the same place. The Friendly Fisherman hadn't returned. She sat down and added a short note to the end of her first letter. Content that her friend would know how she had taken his message to heart, she replaced the jar and hurried home.

An hour later, she waited at the end of the lane as Roman pulled up beside her. His mother sat beside him. "*Guder mariye,* Joann," she called out.

"Good morning, Marie Rose. Have you news of your brother?" Joann climbed into the buggy with them.

"He's doing well and has been moved out of intensive care."

"That is wonderful news."

"Roman tells me you are helping at the printing office again until Otis returns."

She had her old job back, but this wasn't how she wanted it. "Roman has things well in hand. I'm just doing what I can to help."

"We have one more stop to make," Roman said. He seemed out of sorts this morning.

His mother said brightly, "We are picking up Esta Barkman. She wanted to go with me to the hospital after we finish at the school. She's such a thoughtful young woman, and such a good cook, too." She smiled at her son.

Joann wanted to slink away and hide. She hadn't exchanged a single word with Esta since that day in the barn.

Roman turned into the Barkman lane. Esta was waiting on the porch swing. She looked lovely in a crisp new dress of pale lavender. Joann had chosen one of her work dresses to wear. The plain gray fabric and black apron looked shabby next to Esta's cool color.

Esta came down the walk with a wicker basket over her arm. "Hello, everyone. Joann, I'm surprised to see you."

"Roman and I are taking the new books out to the school."

"How kind of you. Very wise to wear your old dress for such work. Isn't she practical, Roman?" She stood beside the buggy looking up at them.

Joann realized they couldn't all sit up front. She got down and climbed in back expecting Esta to sit in back with her.

"*Danki,* Joann." Esta smiled brightly at her and took her place beside Roman's mother up front.

When Roman set the horse in motion, Esta and his mother were engaged in conversation, Joann folded her arms across her chest and stuck her tongue out at Esta's back.

At the publishing office, Joann and Roman loaded the boxes of books while his mother and Esta continued their chat. They were getting ready to leave when Mabel came out with another box of books. "These are some I wanted to donate to the school. They're mostly storybooks and a few songbooks, things I know the kids will enjoy."

Joann put them beside her on the seat. "*Danki,* Mabel. I know Leah will be most grateful."

When they arrived at the school, the work was well under way. A scaffold had been built across the burned opening at the side of the building. Men in straw hats, white shirts and dark pants with suspenders swarmed around the building like ants. Eli Imhoff and Bishop Zook supervised the work and made sure that everyone knew their job.

The sounds of hammers and saws filled the air along with the chatter and laughter of the children who were playing on the school-ground equipment. Long tables had been set up beneath the shade of a nearby tree and women in dark dresses and white *kapps* laid out the food, and made sure everyone had plenty of lemonade or coffee.

Roman's mother and Esta carried their baskets of food toward the tables. Leah came out of the school with Sarah and Sally at her side. "Oh good, you have the books. Bring them inside."

Joann carried the boxes while Roman went to join the men. She and the other women were soon busy shelving books and sorting through the donations that continued to come in.

Later, when they went out to get refreshments, she saw Roman had been put in charge of painting the building. He had seven young boys of various ages wielding paintbrushes beside him. As Joann watched, Esta approached him with a glass of lemonade and a sly smile.

"I can't believe she has set her sights on him again," Sally said as she folded her arms and shook her head.

Joann tried to pretend she didn't care. "His mother likes her. I think she feels it would be a good match."

Sarah stood beside them nibbling on an oatmeal raisin cookie. "I had hoped that you two might hit it off, Joann."

Joann sighed. Sarah always had matchmaking on her mind. "Roman is not my type. He's not sensitive. He doesn't appreciate my quirky sense of humor." She closed her mouth. She had almost revealed her secret.

Sally turned to stare at Joann. "Is there someone who does appreciate your quirky sense of humor?"

Joann couldn't help the blush that heated her cheeks. Sally and Sarah exchanged excited glances and leaned close to Joann. Sarah said, "Out with it. Who is he? Where did you meet him?"

Now she was in a pickle. They both knew something

was up. She was going to have to tell the truth, or some version of the truth.

"I haven't actually met him, but I know a lot about him."

"What does that mean?" Sally asked.

"We've been exchanging letters."

Sarah clapped her hands together. "A pen pal courtship, how wonderful. Who is he? Where does he live?"

Joann shook her head. "I'd rather not say."

Sally's eyes narrowed. "Why not? What is this paragon's name?"

"I'd rather not say," Joann answered in a weak voice.

Sarah nodded. "We won't tease you anymore."

Sally fisted her hands on her hips. "You're making it up."

Joann's chin came up. "I am not."

"Well, there is something fishy about this. How come we haven't heard about him before?"

Joann made sure that no one else was close enough to overhear. "We've been leaving letters for each other in a hollow tree at the lake."

Sarah put her arm around Joann's shoulder. "How romantic."

Sally shook her head. "I'm not buying it."

"It's true," Joann insisted. "I lost my new fishing rod in the lake. I was heartbroken. He went fishing and recovered it. Instead of keeping it, he left it with a note beside it. When I went back to the lake, I found my rod and his note. I wrote him a thank-you letter in the same place. It sort of took off from there."

Sarah's gaze grew troubled. "But you know who he is, right?"

"Not exactly." Joann had never considered how lame it would sound when she tried to explain.

Sally scowled at her. "Are you telling us that you're exchanging letters with a complete stranger who happens to fish at the same lake that you do?"

"That about sums it up. I think I'll have another cookie." She started for the table.

Sally grabbed her arm. "Are you crazy? He could be some kind of nut."

Joann didn't want to hear it. "He's not a nut. He's sensitive and troubled and he shares what he's going through with me. What is so wrong with that?"

Sarah clapped a hand over her mouth. "Oh my goodness. He's *Englisch*."

Joann stared at the ground. "I don't think so. His letters sound…Amish."

"Old Amish? Young Amish? Single Amish? Married Amish? Ex-Amish?" Sally waited for an answer. Joann didn't have one.

"I don't know."

Sarah and Sally each grabbed Joann's arm and pulled her to a more secluded spot. Sarah said, "You don't know his name, but he knows yours. Right?"

"I sign my letters the Happy Angler. He signed his letters the Friendly Fisherman."

"Are you telling us he doesn't even know he's writing to a woman?" Sarah's mouth dropped open.

Joann closed her eyes. "I told him I was an Amish woman. It's only letters. I was afraid he would stop writing if he knew. It started out innocent enough. Why are you making it sound so sordid?"

Sally shook her head. "You have to stop. He could be anybody."

Joann walked a few steps away from them. "You don't understand. We have a connection. I don't want to stop writing him."

"Then you have find out who he is."

"I'm not doing anything wrong. I'm exchanging letters with someone who likes to fish as much as I do.
We share a joke, talk about our problems, offer suggestions and support. There is nothing wrong with what
I'm doing."

Sarah and Sally exchanged pitying glances. Before
they could say anything else, Leah joined them. "It's
almost done. You can't even tell where the fire was.
I'm so thankful for all the people who have come out
today. Come, Bishop Zook is going to offer a blessing."

Sarah and Sally followed her, but Joann stayed where
she was. In her heart, she knew they were right. She
had to end the secrecy. If their friendship was a good
thing, it would bear up in the light of day.

If it didn't, she didn't know what she would do.

Chapter Thirteen

Roman managed to stay busy and out of Esta's reach for most of the day. He was thankful when she and his mother left to visit Otis in the hospital with some of his English friends. Before she got in the car, his mother gave his arm a squeeze. With a happy smile, she said, "It's wonderful to see you and Esta together again."

"We're not together."

His mother leaned closer. "She told me that things have been rough between the two of you, but she's willing to work it out."

Esta was already in the backseat of the car. She had the grace to blush. She scooted over to make room for his mother when she got in. He closed the car door and watched as they drove away. It didn't matter if she charmed his mother or not. He didn't see a future with her.

On the ride home, he glanced frequently at Joann. She seemed deep in thought. A small frown put a crease between her eyebrows. He wanted to smooth it away. "Is something troubling?" he asked.

She glanced at him and shook her head. "I have a hard decision to make and I'm not sure what to do."

"That sounds serious. Is there anything I can do to help?"

"I appreciate the offer, but this is something I have to work out for myself."

"If this is about your job, you can stay on until Otis comes back."

"I will be happy to help out again if you get in a bind, but there isn't enough work to keep all of us busy now that the schoolbooks have been finished. On Monday I'll be at the bookstore again."

"You don't mind?"

She sighed. "I believe everything happens for a reason."

"If only we could see what that reason was." He pulled Meg to a stop at the end of Hebron's lane.

"Then we wouldn't need faith, would we?" she asked gently.

"I reckon not. You don't need to come in Monday unless you really want to. I gave Leonard and Gerald the day off. They've both put in a lot of long hours, and so have you."

She nodded and got down. She paused and turned to face him. "I'm glad that Esta has come to her senses. You two make a nice couple."

"You and my mother," he said in disgust. "I'd like to choose my own wife, if you don't mind."

"I know it isn't any of my business, but I hope you don't hold the things I said in anger against Esta. I was wrong to repeat gossip. I would hate to think that I ruined something between you."

"You didn't ruin anything. You just have a way of making me look at things differently. Good night."

"Good night."

He turned the horse around and drove toward home. As he drew even with the road that led to the lake, he stopped and turned in. He wanted to see if he had a letter. More than that, he wanted to tell his friend about the decisions he'd made.

It took him a while to find the right place. He was used to coming down from the north end of the lake. Once he spotted the faint path leading around the east shore, he left his buggy and walked through the trees.

Roman hoped he might run into his friend on a Saturday evening, but the small glade was empty. There was a note in the jar.

Dear Friendly Fisherman,
I hope your coworker is becoming less of a headache. I think I may have misjudged mine. We are finding our way with each other. I couldn't have done it without you. My mother always used to say a friend is like a rainbow, always there for you after a storm. Thanks, my friend.
A Happy Angler
P.S. I followed your sound advice and searched for my coworker's strengths. I'm happy to say I have discovered that there is much more to him than I first thought. He is committed to taking care of his family, he has a wonderful sense of humor and he is a fine worker. Thank you. Without your wise words, I might have continued to overlook his good qualities and focused only on his failings. I find that I like him a lot.

Roman sat back with a smile. He took out his notebook and pen and wrote.

My Friend,
We really do have a lot in common. How wise God was to put us in touch with each other. I don't see my coworker as a headache anymore. In fact,

I'm finding I like her a lot, too. Much more than
I ever thought I would.

He tapped his lips with the tip of his pen as he decided what else to say.

"I've decided to meet my pen pal."

Joann could barely believe she'd spoken aloud. She
glanced at her cousin Sally to gauge her reaction. Sally
and her family had come for a visit. It was the off Sunday, the one without a church service, and families frequently traveled to visit each other on that day. The
women were gathering morel mushrooms in the woods
beyond the house. Sally's little sister and Joann's nieces
were playing tag up ahead of them.

"Are you sure you want to do that? What if he is
Englisch?" Sally's tone was grave.

Joann walked along with her eyes scanning the
ground. "If he is *Englisch,* well, I can have an *Englisch*
friend."

"Just stop writing him." Sally bent to pick two mo-
rels from the base of a tree.

"You haven't read his letters. We share so many of
the same doubts and hopes. It has nothing to do with
being Amish or being *Englisch.* We're two people trying to find a way to accept God's plan for us."

"I know you feel a connection to this person, but he
may not feel the same connection to you."

"I don't believe that." Joann spotted a small cluster
of mushrooms and moved toward them.

Sally followed her. "Has your pen pal ever suggested
that you meet?"

Joann had trouble meeting Sally's eyes. "No."

Sally stopped and took Joann's hands between her

own. "I am the last person who should be giving any-one advice on matters of the heart, but I'm afraid only heartache will come from this meeting."

"I'm not some giddy teenager. This isn't a matter of the heart."

"Isn't it? Aren't you secretly hoping that your pen pal is a handsome, single man?"

Joann pulled away from Sally. "What if I am?"

"Oh, Joann." Sally shook her head sadly. "He's far more likely to be old, fat, bald and married with a half dozen children or just as many grandchildren."

Tears blurred Joann's vision. "Don't you see? I have to find out. I know that I'm not pretty. I know that I'm not likely to marry. This person respects what I think and how I feel. If it's an Amish grandfather who loves fishing as much as I do, that will be wonderful. We'll be friends and go fishing together as often as possible and I won't feel so lonely."

"And if he should be a handsome, unmarried *Englischer*?"

Joann didn't answer. Both she and Sally knew such a relationship would be forbidden. The only way she could sustain such a relationship would be to leave their Amish community.

Joann turned away from Sally. "I have to know."

She had pined for Levi, but Sarah was the wife God chose for him. Now, she was growing fond of Roman and it seemed that Esta was the one for him.

Joann picked another mushroom and dropped it in her basket. Who was the man for her? "Tomorrow, I'll leave him a note asking to meet."

"If he refuses?"

"I'll stop writing him."

If he agreed to meet, what would happen after that?

* * *

Roman didn't have to go in to work early on Monday, so he made his way to the lake. The Happy Angler frequented their spot in the mornings. He had hopes of running into her today. He wanted to meet his friend in person.

He reached the grove of trees and followed the path toward their fishing hole. He rounded the last bend in the path and stopped in his tracks. A woman was sitting on the fallen log. She had her back to him, but she was dressed plain in a gray dress with a white kapp covering her hair.

He took a step off the path into the cover of the woods. His unknown friend was here? It didn't seem possible.

He checked the area for signs of other people. He didn't see anyone else.

The woman turned around with a jar in her hand. It wasn't a stranger. It was Joann, and she held his letter.

Joann Yoder was the Happy Angler? He couldn't believe it.

She tucked the jar in the hollow of the log and picked up a fishing pole, the very pole he had pulled from the lake a few weeks ago. He was too stunned to move.

He tried to think of everything he had written. Written about her! Not much of it had been flattering. He couldn't quite wrap his mind around the fact that she was the one reading his musings. She really would dunk him in the lake if she found out.

Did she know he was the one reading her letters?

No, he didn't think so. He hadn't said anything specific about himself. He took a step back. He had to think this over. He'd become increasingly fond of Happy Angler. How could she be Joann? He tried to reconcile the two in his mind. He had learned to respect Joann. She had a sharp mind and a fine measure of humor. He'd even started to care about her as a woman, but he wasn't sure she returned such feelings. She practically had him married to Esta, but something in the way she looked at him the other evening gave him hope. He'd seen longing in her eyes, but was it a longing for him?

What would she think when she discovered she had been writing to him all this time?

Would she be pleased or mortified? The last thing he wanted was to cause a new break between them. This was going to take some careful thinking. He needed to be certain how she felt about him before he let on that he was the Friendly Fisherman.

He needed to be certain she *was* the Happy Angler. Maybe she'd simply stumbled on this location and accidentally found the letter jar.

He dropped to a crouch and waited for her to leave. She fished for a while, but didn't catch anything. Soon, she put her rod and tackle box inside the large end of the log and stuffed some grass into the opening.

She hadn't stumbled on this place by accident. He crouched lower as she walked by. When he was certain she had gone, he went to the log and pulled out the jar. His note was gone and there was a brief one in its place.

Dear Friend,
As much as I have enjoyed our correspondences,
I feel it's time we met in person. I have so much
I want to say to you.
Sincerely,
The Happy Angler

The handwriting was the same. Without a doubt, Joann was the one. Someday, he hoped they would look back on these days and laugh about their secret correspondence, but he wasn't laughing yet. He was in trouble.

He pondered how he could make this could come out right as he walked home. The longer he thought about it, the more panicked he became. His brother was crossing the yard. He stopped. "I thought you had gone to work?"

Roman pulled off his hat and raked his fingers through his hair "Not yet. It's her. I couldn't believe my eyes."

"What are you talking about?" His brother looked at him as if he'd gone crazy. Maybe he had.

Roman began pacing. "Joann Yoder."

"I still have no idea what you are talking about."

Roman spun to face him. "I went to the lake today, and she was there. I can't believe this."

"I'm still not following you. Why should you care if Joann Yoder was fishing at the Lake?"

"She wasn't fishing. She was writing a letter."

"I wrote one last month. It's not that amazing that she knows how to do it."

Roman shook his head. "Remember the letter I left for the person whose rod and reel I pulled out of the lake?"

"Sure. He left you a lure as thanks."

"That wasn't the only letter I wrote. We've been exchanging notes ever since, only I thought I was writing to a woman who liked to fish. I never once thought the letters I received came from Joann Yoder."

"Wait a minute. You've been exchanging love letters with Joann Yoder and you didn't know it? What a hoot!" Andrew started laughing.

"They weren't love letters." He began pacing again.

"It's still funny. You and the old maid leaving notes

for each other in a hollow tree. That's priceless. Did she know it was you?"

Andrew's question stopped him. Did she? He found it hard to believe. There hadn't been anything in her demeanor or her notes that suggested she was aware of his identity. "I don't think so."

"I reckon you should tell her the truth. I wouldn't want to be in your shoes when she finds out. She's bound to think it was a prank on your part."

That was exactly what he was afraid of. Roman tried to sort out his feelings. The comforting letters that had sustained him through the past few weeks showed him a completely new side of Joann. He thought he knew her. Now he realized he barely knew her at all. That would have to change, and she would have to get to know him, too.

Andrew chuckled. "I've got to get back to work. Tell me how it turns out. The old maid and you, what a hoot."

After his brother left, Roman went in his house and pulled open the drawer of his desk. He took out the letters Joann had written and began to study them. The sound of a car approaching made him look out the window. The sheriff was getting out of his SUV. Roman went to the door and stepped out on the porch to greet him. "Good day, Nick Bradley. What can we do for you?"

"I stopped by the office. Mable from next door said you had given everyone the day off. I hope everything is okay."

"Everything is fine."

"That's good to hear. I got a copy of your uncle's magazine in the mail this week. It had a license plate number stapled inside. Would you know anything about that?"

"*Ja,* I put it there for you."

"I figured it might be from you. Can you tell me if you know a woman named Jenny Morgan?"

"*Nee.* Who is she? Was she involved in that sad business?"

"I mean to find out if she was involved or not. Thanks for your time, Roman." He touched the brim of his hat, got into his vehicle and drove away.

"What are you reading?"

Joann looked up to find Roman watching her intently. How long had he been standing there?

She was getting ready to start her half day at the bookstore, but she had come to town early so she could stop at the library first. It was such a beautiful summer day that she had decided to read for a few minutes on the bench outside.

She marked her place in the book with the ribbon and closed it. "How are you?"

"Fine. Is it a good book?"

She slipped it into her bag. "I like it."

"Would I like it?" There was something different about his voice today. It was softer, gentler and yet teasing.

Or maybe she was just imagining things. "I doubt it."

"It must be one of those romance novels."

She raised her chin. "There is nothing wrong with a story about two people falling in love."

"I didn't say there was. I believe in love. Who wrote it? Maybe I've even read it." He reached for her book bag. She grabbed the strap. After a brief tug-of-war, he wrestled it away from her.

She crossed her arms and glared at him. "Has anyone told you that you are a bully?"

"Nope." He opened the bag and pulled out her book. His eyes widened in surprise. "Successful Freshwater Bass Fishing. That has to be the most romantic title I've ever heard. Don't tell me how it ends. I have to read it now."

"Ha! Ha!" She snatched the book away from him. He let her take it.

She stuffed the book back in her bag. "Very funny."

"I try. Seriously, I didn't know you liked fishing."

"Everyone likes fishing."

He sat down beside her. "A lot of people like to go fishing, but not a lot of people like to read about it."

"Well, I like to do both." She rose and started walking.

He stood and followed her. "Where are you going?"

"To work."

"I'll walk with you."

She scowled at him. What was wrong with him today? He wore a goofy grin, but he looked nervous.

He fell into step beside her. "Tell me more about the fishing you do."

"Why?"

"You may find this hard to believe, but I enjoy fishing, too."

"What an amazing coincidence!"

"I'm serious. My grandfather used to take me when I was little. I loved sitting on the riverbank beside him and listening to his stories. I didn't even mind if we didn't catch anything."

"Really?" She looked at him in surprise.

"Okay, I enjoyed myself a lot more when the fish were biting."

"That wasn't what I meant. I was just surprised because that's how I learned to love fishing. My grandfather took me with him. He was very old then, and he walked with a cane, but he could look at a stretch of water and tell you right where the fish were. He had a gift. I was named after his wife. I think that's why he liked being with me. Those were the very best days." Joann blinked away the tears in her eyes and hoped Roman hadn't noticed.

He said, "I'm sure he liked being with you because you were a charming child."

She cocked her head to the side. "Now I know you're making fun of me."

"How can you say that?"

"I wasn't a charming child. I was plain." And all but invisible to the people she wanted most to be loved by. Her mother had been sick throughout Joann's childhood. Her father spent all his time caring for her and ignoring his lonely daughter.

"If your grandfather inspired your passion for fishing, who inspired your passion for books?"

"I'm not sure. As soon as I learned to read it was like the entire world opened up and invited me in. I could read about places that are far away, have adventures along with the people in the stories. I was hooked."

"I didn't discover books until I started working for Otis. He opened my eyes to what books can do for people."

"That's what I loved about working for him. How is he?"

"Doing well. He should be out of the hospital by the end of the week."

"That's great."

By this time they had reached the printing office. Roman held the door open for her. She said, "I'm working at the bookstore today."

"Oh, right. Say, my brother and I sometimes go fishing. Maybe you can join us one of these days."

"Sure." She smiled and turned away. He was just being polite. She knew the trip would never materialize.

"Great. I'll see you tomorrow." He went into the office and closed the door.

A second later, the door popped open again. He leaned out and said, "I mean it, teacher. We'll go fishing soon."

She giggled and nodded. "Okay, soon."

She spent the rest of the day smiling as she worked. Her heart was warmed by his thoughtfulness.

Chapter Fourteen

On Saturday afternoon, Joann was on her hands and knees sweeping paper shreds from beneath the largest press when she heard her name called in a secretive whisper. She looked behind her to see Sally peeking under the press.

"How did it go? Your meeting with your pen pal. How did it go? Is he fat and bald?"

Joann crawled out and stood up. "I have no idea. He hasn't been back or at least he hasn't left another letter. Why are you whispering?"

Sally looked around then took a step closer. "Believe me, Joann, exchanging secret letters with a total stranger is not the kind of thing you want getting out. Do you think he's avoiding you?"

Joann shrugged. "I have no idea."

"What are you going to do?"

"Finish cleaning this press and then mop the floors."

Sally wrinkled her nose. "Don't be smart. I mean about your mystery guy."

"There isn't much I can do except wait for him to contact me."

"I'm going to go crazy if he doesn't do it soon."

Joann had trekked to the lake and back every morning for the past six days. "How do you think I feel? Maybe he's just busy."

"Maybe his wife found out. Maybe he fell in the lake and drowned. Maybe he read the note and moved to Montana."

Joann rolled her eyes. "Sally, stop it."

Her cousin pointed a finger at her. "This is all your fault."

"Go home. I've got work to do."

"You'll tell me as soon as you hear from him, right?"

"I promise."

Sally tipped her head to one side as she studied Joann. "Is that a new dress? I've never seen you in that color before. It's nice. Mauve suits you."

"Danki." Joann smoothed the front of her matching apron. Sally waved as she headed for the door. Joann waved back. When she was alone, she spun around once to make the skirt flare out. It was a pretty color. She knew it was vain, but she hoped Roman would notice and like it, too.

When Joann finished her work and left the building, she found Roman waiting outside the office in his buggy with Andrew beside him.

Roman jumped down. "Good afternoon. My brother and I are on our way to do some fishing. I thought I'd swing by and see if you wanted to join us."

"Now?"

"Ja. We're going to a creek not far from here."

"I know you said you would invite me soon, but I wasn't expecting this soon."

Roman smiled at her. "It was a last-minute decision on my part. I understand if you're busy and don't want to come."

Of course, I want to come. Don't read more into this than it is, Joann. He's asking me to go fishing, like I'm one of the boys. He's not asking me out on a date.

She struggled to hide her excitement. "I'd like to go, but I don't have a pole."

"That's okay. We have an extra rod. Come on, it will be fun."

She looked at his brother. "Andrew, are you sure you don't mind?"

"I'm just along for the ride. This is Roman's idea."

Roman scowled at him. "He doesn't mind a bit."

Andrew shrugged. "Okay, I don't mind."

Roman waited and watched silently as she struggled with her decision. If he pushed any harder, he knew she would refuse. Andrew wasn't helping anything. He'd have a thing or two to say to him when they got home.

Gaining Joann's trust was what Roman was after, but he had to take it one small step at a time.

She nodded and said, "*Ja,* I reckon I could go for a little while."

He could have jumped for joy, but instead he said, "Fine. Hop in."

Andrew drove as they headed east out of town. A half mile later, they pulled off to the side of the road and tethered the horse, then, the three of them left the buggy and walked across the field to a shady spot on the creek.

The bank was grassy, green and inviting beneath a grove of a maple trees. Roman saw the way Joann relaxed once she had a pole in her hand. He was happy to sit on the bank and watch her while pretending to keep an eye on his cork. Andrew moved farther downstream to try his luck there and to give them some privacy.

Roman said, "There's nothing better than a day spent fishing, if you ask me."

She was studying the rod holder strapped to his leg. "Do you mind if I ask what that is for?"

"Not at all. This is Andrew's invention. It holds my rod so I can crank with one hand."

"How interesting. I'd like to see it in action."

"You will if the fish cooperate."

Joann's cork went under. He sat up. "You've got one."

She jumped to her feet and set the hook. The tip of her rod bent nearly double. Her reel screeched as the fish took more line and ran with it.

Roman was on his feet beside her. "Andrew, bring the net!"

Joann laughed aloud. She hadn't had so much fun in ages. "He's a big one. I don't think I can hold him."

"Yes, you can. Don't let the line go slack. He'll snap it if you do. Work him toward the bank." Roman coached her along.

She managed to crank in a small amount of line. "I'm trying."

Andrew arrived with a dip net. "Wow, you've hooked a monster."

Roman took the net from him and moved to the edge of the bank. "Bring him a little closer."

Joann pulled with all her might, backing up to bring the fish within his reach. He leaned out over the water. She said, "Roman, be careful. You'll fall in."

"Don't worry about me. Land your fish."

She fought on with both men shouting encouragement. Each time she got the fish close to the bank, it darted out again into deeper water.

By this time, Andrew was behind Roman holding on

to the waistband of his pants to keep his brother from tumbling headlong into the stream. The fish finally surfaced. Andrew shouted, "It's a carp."

"And a mighty big one," Roman added.

Joann's arms were getting tired. "I could've told you that. Get him in the net or he's going to get away."

The fish was running out of steam. She pulled him closer. Roman leaned out as far as he could. Suddenly, the lip of the bank gave way. Roman fell and pulled Andrew in with him.

Joann shrieked. Roman came up with a net in his hand and the fish safely in the net. His straw hat went floating downstream. Joann sat in the grass and laughed until tears ran down her face. Andrew waded after Roman's hat and pulled it out of the water. He was grinning from ear to ear.

As the two men struggled out of the creek, she pressed a hand to her mouth. "All that for a poor old carp that isn't good to eat anyway."

The men didn't seem to care. They were admiring the size of their prize. Andrew said, "I reckon he's twenty-five pounds."

"At least," Roman agreed. He smiled brightly at her.

Joann's heart took a funny leap. No one had ever smiled at her that way. She couldn't help herself. She had to glance behind her to see if he was looking at someone else. No one was there. She turned back to him. He wasn't looking through her. He was looking right at her with those shining blue eyes that put the sky to shame.

In that instant, she realized she was falling hard for Roman and she had no idea what to do about it.

She gloried in the feeling for a heartbeat and then reality reared its ugly head. She was doomed to love in vain. Someone like Roman would never fall for someone like her.

Joann's practical side quickly asserted itself. "We need to get you guys home and out of those wet things."

"Reckon you're right." Roman seemed reluctant to call a halt to the day.

"Put my poor fish back in the creek. He's gasping already."

Roman carried the carp to the water's edge. Andrew said, "I kinda hate to put him back after all the trouble we went to catch him."

She had to agree, but she would be forever grateful to the silver beauty for showing her how wonderful love could feel, if only for a little while.

When they arrived back at Hebron's farm an hour later, Roman got out and walked with her to the door.

She said, "Thanks for taking me fishing. I had a great time."

"So did I. Are you doing anything tomorrow evening?"

She gave him a puzzled look. "Nothing special, why?"

"I thought you might enjoy going on a picnic after church services. The weather is supposed to be nice."

Was he serious? "A picnic? With you?"

"Ja."

"And who else?" She could understand the invitation if it was to a party.

"No one. Just you and I."

She didn't dare hope that he returned her affections. What was he up to? "Why?"

"Joann, I enjoy your company when we aren't trading insults. What do you say?"

Was he making fun of her? He looked perfectly serious, worried even, as if he were afraid she would say no. "Did Sarah put you up to this?"

He shook his head. "No one put me up to it. If you don't want to go, just say so. I will be disappointed, but I'll live."

"You really want to take me on a picnic?" Joy began to spread through her body.

"I do."

A giddy sensation she hadn't felt since she was a teenager made her smile. "I reckon a picnic sounds like fun."

He smiled brightly. "Great. I'll pick you up at noon, if that's okay with you?"

"Noon will be fine. What shall I bring?"

"Just yourself." He stood there smiling at her, looking so handsome it made her heart ache.

She said, "You should get home. Andrew looks miserable."

"You're right. See you tomorrow." He tipped his hat, climbed into his buggy and drove away.

Joann wasn't sure if she actually touched the floor when she went inside her brother's home. Roman Weaver had asked her to go out with him. Just him. No one else. She had a date.

She felt like singing, like spinning in circles until she fell to the floor, too dizzy to move. She was going on a picnic with Roman.

She ate her supper without tasting a thing. That night, she lay in bed unable to sleep as anticipation chased sleep away. It was a long time before she finally closed her eyes and slept.

She was awake before dawn brightened the sky. Her giddiness had vanished in the night. What was she thinking? Why had she agreed to go? She was barreling toward heartache. He couldn't possibly care for someone like her.

He must have been joking. He wouldn't come at noon. He wouldn't show up at all. She'd made a terrible mistake by agreeing to go. Right now, he and his brother were sitting somewhere laughing at her gullibility.

When twelve o'clock finally arrived, Hebron came in from finishing his chores. Joann helped her sister-in-law prepare lunch. She was setting the table when Salome burst in. "Aunt Joann, there's someone here to see you."

Joann stopped breathing. "Who is it?"

"It's Roman Weaver." Salome's eyes danced with excitement. "He's driving a courting buggy."

Hebron scowled at Joann. "Why has he come to see you?"

She smoothed the front of her apron to hide her trembling hands. "He's taking me on a picnic."

"Is he really?" Salome demanded.

"*Ja,* he really is." She looked at her sister-in-law. "I don't expect to be back until late, so don't wait supper on me."

Everyone was staring at her with their mouths open. Joann pulled her book bag off the hook by the door and rushed outside before her courage failed.

Roman slipped a finger under the collar of his shirt to loosen it. He hadn't been this nervous since…ever. It occurred to him that he was rushing things, but he didn't want to keep the truth from Joann a moment longer. He had come to care deeply for her. He wanted their relationship to be based on trust and understanding. He wanted to be more than her friend. Much more.

As she came out the door, she gave him a beautiful

smile. His heart flipped over in his chest and started beating like mad. She took his breath away.

She slid in beside him in the buggy. "What a glorious day."

"It sure is." It wasn't the weather that filled him with happiness. It was having her beside him.

"Any ill effects?" Her voice sounded breathy and nervous. Her cheeks were pink and her eyes sparkled. He sure hoped he was the reason.

"From what?"

She giggled. "Your swim with the fishes."

"*Nee,* I'm fine and so is Andrew. We'll have to do that again."

She looked down at her hands. "I'd like that. Where are we going?"

"I thought we might go out to the lake."

Her head snapped up. She stared at him with wide eyes. "The lake?"

Suddenly, it didn't seem like such a great plan. "If that's okay with you?"

"It's okay. *Ja,* it's fine. I like going to the lake."

"So do I. It's peaceful there."

She fell silent, and he drove the rest of the way with growing misgivings.

When they reached the south shore, he parked in the shade of an oak tree. She said, "This is a good spot. Shall I put the blanket out here?"

"No, it's prettier on the east side of the lake. Let's take our stuff over there."

Some of the joy left her eyes. "Okay."

He hated that he was tricking her, but he had arranged for the Friendly Fisherman to introduce himself. It had seemed so clever when he thought of it. He prayed he was doing the right thing. He took the picnic basket from the back of the buggy and started following the path around the lake. When they reached the clearing with the fallen tree, he looked down at her. "I like this spot, don't you?"

She relaxed a little. "It's fine."

He said, "You put out our things. I left the lemonade in the buggy. I'll be right back."

Joann couldn't believe Roman had brought her to the same spot where she exchanged letters with her secret friend. Once he was out of sight, she laid open the blanket and went to the log. Reaching into the knothole, she brought out her mail jar. There was a new note inside. She opened the lid and took it out.

My dear friend,
I would be delighted to meet you face to face. We do have a lot to talk about. So turn around.
F.F.

Turn around. Her heart skipped a beat and stumbled onward. Slowly, she looked up. Roman was standing at the edge of the trees. He lifted his hand in a brief wave. "Hi."

A terrible buzzing filled her ears. This couldn't be happening. He hadn't brought her here for a picnic. He'd brought her here to humiliate her. She should have known better. What a fool she was.

She pressed a hand to her forehead. "It was you! All this time I thought I was reading heartfelt letters from some stranger. Only I wasn't. I was the victim of your sick joke."

He took a step toward her. "No, Joann, it wasn't like that."

She was so embarrassed she thought she might die from shame. When she thought of the things she had confided to him it made her ill. "Did you know it was me all along?"

"Of course not."

"You knew before today, didn't you?"

"I couldn't tell you. I wasn't sure you even liked me."

He knew and he'd said nothing. How humiliating. "I have a newsflash for you, Roman Weaver. I still don't like you. You are mean and underhanded and dishonest. I can't believe I ever thought I did like you. Never speak to me again."

Joann dashed past him and began running through the trees. She heard him calling, but she didn't slow down. She ran past his buggy and across the pasture until she was so out of breath that she had to stop and lean against the gate.

What an idiot she was. He must be laughing his head off. Tears blinded her. She wiped them away. "I don't cry. I never cry."

Only today, she did.

Roman couldn't believe how things had gone from so good to so bad in a heartbeat. He gathered up the remains of their picnic and followed Joann. She had to listen to him. He had to make her understand that he had been afraid of losing her friendship. Only now, it seemed that he'd lost so much more.

She wasn't waiting at the buggy. He repeatedly called her name, but she didn't answer

So much for his bright idea. He left the lake and drove to her brother's house. She wasn't there. She hadn't come back and they didn't know where she might be.

Defeated, Roman went home. Perhaps if he gave her enough time, she would cool off and be able to see that he did care for her.

The next day, he waited impatiently for her to come to work. She didn't show up. He started to worry. He left work early and went back to her brother's house only to be told she still hadn't come home. No one in the family had seen her.

Where could she be? Who would she seek out? Sally perhaps?

He set his tired horse in motion once more and drove out to Sally's home.

Sally was hanging clothes on the line when he drove in the yard. He left the buggy and crossed the lawn with long strides. "Is she here?"

Sally looked at him as if he were crazy. "Is who here?"

"I don't want to play games. Is Joann here?

"She is not. What's going on?"

"I need to speak to her. I need to make her understand that I care about her. I hurt her without meaning to."

"How?"

Roman hesitated but finally explained what had been going on. Sally was every bit as upset as Joann had been. "You weasel. First, you take her job, she loses the home she's always wanted and then you toy with her affections. I wouldn't want to see you again either."

"Wait a minute. What do you mean I took her job?"

"Her job at the newspaper. She was fired so you could have it. Did you really think she only wanted to clean up after you?"

"I thought it was odd, but she said it was what she wanted."

"No, the job you could care less about is the job she wanted. The job she needed."

"So she could buy a house of her own," he said softly, remembering her letter.

Sally's attitude softened. "You really didn't know?"

"That my uncle put her on the cleaning staff so that I could have her job? No. It never crossed my mind."

"Not only did you get her job, she had to teach you how do it. It wasn't fair of Otis Miller to do that."

"No wonder she seemed to resent me. How can I make this right? I do care about her. You must believe me."

"To start with, you're gonna have to eat a lot of crow."

"I can't tell her how sorry I am if I can't find her. Do you know where she is?"

"Maybe I do, and maybe I don't. If you are sincere about patching things up with her, I'll see what I can do to help."

The truth dawned on him in a blinding flash. "Sally, not only am I sincere about patching things up with her, I want her to be my wife. And I don't care who knows it."

"Well, that puts a slightly different slant on things. Okay, I'll help, but you have to go home now."

"Go home? I can't. Not until I've talked to her."

"Men are so clueless sometimes. You have to give her a little cooling-off time. Joann is a smart woman, but she doesn't have a lot of confidence. She's felt unwanted most of her life. Thinking that someone loves her for herself is not something that she's used to doing. Give her some time to let the idea sink in. If she still isn't willing to talk to you in a few days' time, then drastic measures will be needed."

He didn't like the sound of that. "What kind of drastic measures?"

"Nothing for you to worry about. Go home and wait until I contact you. Trust me."

He didn't want to go home. He wanted to find Joann and make her understand how much he loved her, but it didn't look like that would happen tonight. It was with a heavy heart that he left and drove away.

When he arrived at the sawmill, he saw the sheriff talking to his father. Andrew came and took the horse from Roman. "The sheriff wants to talk to you."

"All right."

Roman walked toward the sheriff and his father. "How can I help you, Nick Bradley?"

"I came to let you know we arrested someone for the arson at the school and for the vandalism at your uncle's business."

"Who?"

"Robert Smith, Brendan's younger brother. The woman who came by the printing office after the attack is his girlfriend. The farmer out on Bent Tree Road was able to give me a description of the car they saw speeding away. When I ran the license plate number I received in the mail, her name came up. Her car matched the description of the one at the haystack fire. When I confronted her, she told me everything."

Roman shoved his hands in his pockets. "Did she say why?"

"She thought they were having some harmless fun. They were getting their kicks out of torching a few haystacks. It wasn't until Robert wanted to burn down the school that she started getting worried. She was the one who called in the tip to us that day. After Otis was hurt, she got scared and broke it off with Robert."

"Why does he hate us so?" Menlo asked.

"She said he hates the Amish because they won't fight for their country. He tried to join the Army, but he was rejected. He thinks the Amish are a bunch of hypocrites."

Shame filled Roman. "If I had asked for leniency for his brother, maybe none of this would've happened."

"In my book, Brendan got what he deserved. He didn't know and he didn't care that you were standing at the side of the road when he sideswiped you. He thought it would be funny to knock the door off your buggy because the Amish don't report crimes to the law. Usually. This time you stopped a crime, Roman. According to Jenny, Robert was planning to torch this place next."

Menlo laid a hand on Roman's shoulder. "God was merciful to us."

The sheriff nodded. "I just wanted you to know that the people around here are safer thanks to you."

As Sheriff Bradley walked away, Roman called after him, "Sheriff, will you do me a favor?"

"If I can. What is it?"

"Will you tell the attorney for Brendan and his brother that I will be pleased to come speak on their behalves? Forgiveness is about more than words. It has taken me a while to understand that."

The sheriff nodded and smiled. "I'll be happy to pass on the message."

Chapter Fifteen

Joann sat on the window seat of Sarah's old house and watched the activity on the street below. She was grateful that Sarah and Levi had allowed her to stay in the empty house. Levi had brought over a cot for her to sleep on. It was all she needed at the moment. A place to hide until her heartache healed.

A buggy pulled up in front of Levi's shop and her cousin Sally stepped out. Tears pricked Joann's eyes. She didn't want to see anybody. She hoped that Sarah wouldn't reveal where she was.

Her hope was in vain. Only a few minutes after entering Levi's shop, Sally emerged with Sarah and they both crossed the street toward her.

She heard the front door open downstairs. Sally's voice called out, "Joann, are you here?"

Maybe if she stayed silent, they would go away. She should've known better. Sally came tromping up the stairs. "I know you're up here, Joann. Answer me."

"Joann doesn't live here anymore. She ran away and joined the circus."

The bedroom door flew open and Sally breezed in. "I've often thought that being an Amish circus performer would be a truly difficult way to live. But if that's what you want, I'll support you."

Joann sighed. "Go away, Sally. I don't want to talk to anyone."

Sally sat beside her on the window bench. "So don't talk, just listen."

Sarah came into the bedroom and stood with her arms folded. "Don't bully her, Sally."

Sally sat back. "You're right. I am trying to bully her into believing that she is a terrific person and that any man would be blessed to have her be part of his life. Even Roman Weaver."

Joann said, "I appreciate the sentiment, but that is hardly the case. I'm a sad, pathetic excuse of a woman who fell in love with an idea, not with a real man."

Sally said, "I have to admit that he's not much of a catch. Who would want a man who can't hold you in his arms?"

Joann glared at Sally. "He only needs one good arm to put around me. If he lost both arms he would still be smarter and more determined than any man I know."

Sally smiled. "That's a pretty strong defense of someone you don't see as a real man."

"You know what I mean."

Sarah came and sat down on the other side of Joann. "I only have one question for you. Do you love him?"

"How can I love someone who lies to me, who tricks me into thinking that he is something he's not?"

Sarah took Joann's hands in her own. "That wasn't exactly a no."

"Okay, I love him, but that doesn't change anything."

"She's right," Sally said. "We just have to figure out what to do now."

Joann stood and crossed the room before turning to face them. "I've come to a decision."

"Not the circus," Sally said dryly.

"No, not the circus. I have an aunt who lives near Bird-in-Hand, Pennsylvania. She left the Amish years ago. My brothers have forbidden anyone to speak about her, but I believe she'll take me in. I'm family, after all."

Sally slapped her hands on her knees. "Wonderful. Now that that's taken care of, all you have to do is write her and wait for an answer."

Joann frowned at her. "Are you that eager to be rid of me?"

"Of course not," Sarah said. "We just want what is best for you."

Sally stood. "In the meantime, we need to get you a pair of new dresses. You can't go to her looking like a pauper. I'll bring some material over tomorrow and we can get you ready to start a new and different life. Wow, I envy you that."

Sally's eyes grew sad. Before Joann could ask her what was wrong, she perked up and said, "I'll be back first thing tomorrow morning."

She charged out of the room, but Sarah remained. "Joann, you are welcome to stay with Levi and me for as long as you like. I hope you know that."

"I appreciate that, Sarah, but I need to move on with my life. There isn't anything for me here."

"I think you're wrong about that, but I'll accept whatever decision you make."

Sarah left and Joann was alone again.

Roman was almost out of patience.

Sally had told him to have faith and wait until she contacted him, but it had been a week and there was still no sign of Joann. Each day he grew more afraid that he had lost her forever. He was proofreading an article for the magazine when the front door of the shop opened. He looked up hoping it was Joann, but it was finally Sally.

"It's about time. Where is she?" he demanded.

Sally gave him a look of disgust. "I have no idea what she sees in you."

"I'm sorry. Hello, Sally, how may I help you?" He forced a smile to his stiff lips.

"You need to go fishing right now."

"Is this some kind of joke, because if it is…" His voice trailed off. He was in no position to issue an ultimatum and she knew it.

"Joann is packed and ready to go to her aunt's home in Pennsylvania. Her aunt's letter arrived today. She wants to leave on this evening's bus. All that she's lacking is her fishing pole. She went to collect."

"To her brother, Hebron's place?"

Sally shook her head. "He's the one who threw it in the lake. Long story. She said she kept it in a hollow log at the lake. Since that was where you exchanged letters, I assume you know where she is going."

He got up from his desk and grabbed his hat. "I could kiss you, Sally."

"Yuck. Not interested. You should hurry. She left Sarah's home thirty minutes ago."

When Roman reached the lake he prayed he wasn't too late. He rounded the last bend in the path and held his breath.

She was sitting on the fallen log by the edge of the water. For a moment, he was too scared to speak. What if he couldn't make her understand? What if he had to spend the rest of his life without her?

Unless he could convince her of his love, that was exactly what would happen.

He prayed for the strength and wisdom to say what

she needed to hear. Suddenly, a deep calm came over him. He knew in his heart that she was the woman God had chosen for him. He took a deep breath and walked into the clearing. "Are they biting today?"

She tensed but didn't look at him. "I don't know."

At least she wasn't running away. He took a seat a few feet away from her on a log.

"What do you want, Roman?" There was so much pain in her voice that he wanted to wrap his arm around her and hold her close, but he knew that would be a mistake.

"I want you to be happy, Joann. I know you don't believe that, but it's the truth."

"You hurt me." Her voice quivered.

"I know, and I am so sorry."

She crossed her arms and raised her chin. "If you have come seeking my forgiveness, I give it freely."

He chose his words carefully. "I didn't come seeking forgiveness."

For the first time she looked at him. "Then why are you here?"

"Because you are here. No matter where I go, I'm lonely if I'm not with you."

She bowed her head. Her voice was barely more than a whisper. "Stop pretending. I'm not the kind of woman a man like you falls for."

How could he make her understand? He moved to stand in front of her and then dropped to his knees. "Oh, sweet Joann, you are exactly the kind of woman I have fallen for. I need you."

"Don't," she whispered, turning her face away.

"I have to say this and you have to hear it. I need someone smart and steadfast who will overlook my mistakes. I need someone kind and patient, someone who can teach me to be a better man. I need you, my darling teacher."

She looked down at her clenched hands. "You could have your pick of the pretty girls for miles around. You don't have to settle for someone like me."

"Why would I want a pretty girl when I have a beautiful woman right in front of me?"

"I may be a lot of things, but I'm not beautiful."

"I know you don't think you are, but my eyes see the face of an angel when I look at you. If you would but smile at me, my heart would be made whole again."

"I don't believe you." She started to rise, but he grabbed her hand.

"What can I say that will make you believe me?"

"Nothing."

He let go and sank back on his heels. "Is it because I'm crippled?"

"Don't be ridiculous, Roman."

"How is it ridiculous to lay open my heart and then have you trod on it?"

He rose to his feet and walked to the edge of the water. With his head bowed, he said, "If my disability repels you, I can accept that."

He felt the touch of her hand on his back. He turned to face her.

Joann had never been more confused and more frightened in her life. Here was everything she wanted and everything she knew she could never have. "I don't find you repulsive. No woman could."

"Then why won't you marry me?"

She bit her lip and looked down. "I'm not the marrying kind. I was born to be an old maid."

He put his finger under her chin and forced her to

look at him. "For such an intelligent woman, that is the stupidest thing I've ever heard you say."

There were tears in his eyes. It broke her heart to see him in pain. "It's true."

"No, the truth is that I love you and you love me. You're just afraid to say it."

He was right. She was terrified. What if he changed his mind? What if he realized what a poor bargain she really was? How could she face loving him and losing him?

He kissed her cheek. "Be brave, my darling, Joann. You were chosen by God to be my mate. Have faith in God's mercy. Believe that I love you, that I vow before God to love, honor, and cherish you my entire life. Please, I beg you, say that you love me, too."

How could she refuse him anything? She searched her soul and found the faith and courage she needed. She closed her eyes and took a plunge into the unknown. "All right. I love you, Roman Weaver."

He cupped her cheek with his hand and kissed her gently. He drew back and gazed into her eyes. "You have made me the happiest man in the world."

She smiled as he pulled her close and wrapped his arm around her. Her arms moved up to circle his neck. It felt so right and so wonderful to hold him. It was like a marvelous dream and she was very much afraid she would wake up to find it wasn't true.

"Tell me the truth, Joann. Does it bother you that I only have one arm to hold you with?"

She pulled back a little so that she could see his face. "*Nee,* it does not bother me. What bothers me is that someday you may not wish to hold me."

"That day will never come."

"How can you be so sure?"

"How can you be sure the sun will rise tomorrow?"

"I guess I can't be. I just have faith that it will."

"Then I ask that you have faith in me, too, for I will love you until the day I die."

"Oh, Roman, what have I done to deserve such joy?"

"I don't know, but I am ever thankful that God has smiled upon us."

She looked out over the waters of the lake. "I'm going to miss coming here to read your letters."

"I don't see why we have to stop writing each other. Our wedding won't be until late November."

"Our wedding. That has a wonderful sound to it."

"It does, doesn't it? Mrs. Roman Weaver. I like the sound of that, too."

She laid her head against his chest. "Mrs. Roman Weaver. I *love* the sound that. You know what's funny?"

"What?"

"Sarah told me that we would be a good match." She looked up at him and smiled.

He kissed the tip of her nose. "Remind me to thank her."

"What is your favorite kind of pie?"

"I like them all, but I guess I would have to say my favorite is pumpkin."

"Pumpkin. I like pumpkin pie. That will be easy enough."

"Do I want to know why you're asking that question?"

"Levi said the way to a man's heart is through his stomach. That looks fade but good cooking never does."

"Obviously, he doesn't know what he's talking about. I've never tasted your cooking. You found the way to my heart with pen and ink and a fishing rod."

She chuckled. "I thought the Friendly Fisherman was an ancient Amish grandfather who shared his wisdom with me. What did you think the Happy Angler was like?"

Suddenly she stepped away from him and fisted her hand on her hips. "You said I was someone who would benefit from a dunking in the lake. That I was stubborn, willful, hard to please, and quick to call attention to your failings."

He reached out and pulled her back against him. "And what part of that isn't true? Be honest, soon-to-be Mrs. Roman Weaver."

"I'm not stubborn."

"Yes, you are, and I love that about you."

"I'm not hard to please."

"Have you ever considered marrying anyone else in Hope Springs?"

"No."

"There are a lot of nice fellows hereabouts. Do you agree?"

She nodded. "There are some nice boys around here."

"And yet you have only agreed to marry me. Therefore, you are hard to please, but you knew that and waiting for the right man to come along was worth the wait."

"You have yet to prove that you are worth the wait."

He cupped the back of her head and leaned down until his forehead rested against hers. "Then I had best get started, hadn't I?"

"*Ja,* you should," she answered and gladly raised her face for his kiss.

A long time later, Roman pulled his horse to a stop in front of Sarah and Levi's home. Joanne hated to see the day end, but she knew it had to

"I'm glad I had the chance to live in Sarah's house before it was sold."

Roman studied her for a moment. "Is this the house you wanted to buy?"

"This is the one." She smiled at him. "But I will enjoy living anywhere you are."

"I've been thinking about that. My arm may not ever be better than it is now. My younger brother can handle the sawmill with my dad. Otis would like me to take over his business when the time comes."

"You do a wonderful job there."

He leaned close and kissed her nose. "I had a good teacher."

She blushed and laid her head on his shoulder. "There are many things that we will learn together. How to raise children, how to bring them up to value our way of life, how to grow old together."

"As long as I learn those lessons with you by my side, I will be a content man. Will you work with me at the printing office until our children arrive?"

"Gladly." Her heart turned over with happiness at his request. What could be better than working at his side?

"*Goot,* for I need my teacher and my friend beside me."

"I will always be there for you, my love."

"If I'm going to be working in town for the rest of my life, I'm thinking I may need to buy a house that's closer to where I work. Any suggestions?"

Joann wrapped her arms around his and squeezed. "I know the perfect house, and it's for sale."

"Only God is perfect, my love."

She looked up into the eyes of the most wonderful man she would ever meet. The man God had chosen for her. "It may not be perfect, but with you there, the fence painted white, pansies along the walk, our children playing there and a birdhouse in the corner of the yard, it will be very, very close."

* * * * *

Dear Reader,

Didn't this book make you want to grab a pole and head to your favorite fishing spot? Okay, maybe not, unless you knew people like Roman and Joann would be there, too. I don't need any excuse to grab my pole. I love fishing. Here in Kansas, our lakes and ponds supply wonderful fishing for bass, perch, bluegill, catfish, wipers, stripers and, yes, the occasional enormous carp.

I'm not the only one in my family who enjoys fishing. My dad is always eager to take the boat out on the lake. Just a reminder, never take the boat out without an oar in it. Yes, I have had to paddle back in more than once. Life is always an adventure. My brother Mark is a fly-fishing guide in Montana. Now, that is fun with beautiful scenery thrown in.

Enough about me and my hobby. I know you're wondering what's next for the folks in Hope Springs, Ohio. I'm happy to say that I have another Christmas story coming up. Leah, the schoolteacher, is about to be reunited with the man who broke her sister's heart and left her pregnant. He hasn't come back alone. He has an eight-year-old daughter with Down syndrome who will be attending Leah's school. Can his special-needs daughter help him heal the wounds he left behind?

I can't wait to find out.

Blessings to you and yours,

Patricia Davids

Questions for Discussion

1. Was Otis Miller right to give Joann's job to his nephew? Why or why not?

2. Do you enjoy fishing? If you have never been, why not?

3. What is your fondest childhood memory of your grandfather?

4. Joann's brothers were attempting to be fair when they made her living arrangements. Has someone in your family made the same mistake of thinking they know what is best? How did you deal with the situation?

5. Joann was caught up in the excitement of maintaining a secret correspondence. Is it easier to explore your feelings about someone in writing or in person?

6. What character did you identify with most in this book?

7. What part of this story did you enjoy the most? Why?

8. What part of the book didn't you like, and why?

9. Joann longs for a home of her own. How is this an analogy for what is wrong with her life?

10. Were you surprised to learn that the Amish have their own printing companies?

11. Roman was unable to accept his disability. Have you or someone you know had to face similar trials?

12. The Amish have been subjected to persecution since the beginning of their religion. In what way can we foster acceptance of religious beliefs other than our own?

13. Which characters in Hope Springs would you be interested in learning more about?

14. Were you surprised to learn that some Amish communities take up annual collections for road repair and use?

15. Every year, Amish men, women and children are killed or injured in automobile versus buggy collisions. What would you suggest we do to make their lives safer?

COMING NEXT MONTH from Love Inspired®
AVAILABLE JUNE 18, 2013

LOVE IN BLOOM
The Heart of Main Street
Arlene James

With the help of handsome widowed rancher Tate Bronson and his little girl-turned-matchmaker, can Lily Farnsworth create a garden of community and love deep in the heart of Kansas...and one special man?

BABY IN HIS ARMS
Whisper Falls
Linda Goodnight

When helicopter pilot Creed Carter finds an abandoned baby on a church altar, he must convince foster parent Haley Blanchard that she'll make a good mom—and a good match.

NOAH'S SWEETHEART
Lancaster County Weddings
Rebecca Kertz

Noah Lapp captures Rachel Hostetler's heart from the moment he rescues her from a runaway buggy, but he's expected to marry Rachel's cousin. Too bad the heart doesn't always follow plans....

MONTANA WRANGLER
Charlotte Carter

When Paige Barclay suddenly becomes guardian to her nephew, she finds herself clashing with ranch foreman Jay Red Elk over what's best for the boy. Will these stubborn hearts ever fall in love?

SMALL-TOWN MOM
Jean C. Gordon

Nurse Jamie Glasser has managed to shut all things military out of her life. But former army captain Eli Payton can help her troubled son—if Jamie will let him in.

HIS UNEXPECTED FAMILY
Patricia Johns

As police chief, Greg Taylor has the task of delivering an orphaned infant to the care of Emily Shaw. He never expected to become wrapped around this baby's heart—or her mother's.

LICNM0613

REQUEST YOUR FREE BOOKS!

2 FREE INSPIRATIONAL NOVELS
PLUS 2
FREE
MYSTERY GIFTS

Love Inspired

YES! Please send me 2 FREE Love Inspired® novels and my 2 FREE mystery gifts (gifts are worth about $10). After receiving them, if I don't wish to receive any more books, I can return the shipping statement marked "cancel." If I don't cancel, I will receive 6 brand-new novels every month and be billed just $4.74 per book in the U.S. or $5.24 per book in Canada. That's a saving of at least 21% off the cover price. It's quite a bargain! Shipping and handling is just 50¢ per book in the U.S. and 75¢ per book in Canada.* I understand that accepting the 2 free books and gifts places me under no obligation to buy anything. I can always return a shipment and cancel at any time. Even if I never buy another book, the two free books and gifts are mine to keep forever.

105/305 IDN F47Y

Name _____ (PLEASE PRINT) _____

Address _____ Apt. #

City _____ State/Prov. _____ Zip/Postal Code

Signature (if under 18, a parent or guardian must sign)

Mail to the Harlequin® Reader Service:
IN U.S.A.: P.O. Box 1867, Buffalo, NY 14240-1867
IN CANADA: P.O. Box 609, Fort Erie, Ontario L2A 5X3

**Are you a subscriber to Love Inspired books
and want to receive the larger-print edition?
Call 1-800-873-8635 or visit www.ReaderService.com.**

* Terms and prices subject to change without notice. Prices do not include applicable taxes. Sales tax applicable in N.Y. Canadian residents will be charged applicable taxes. Offer not valid in Quebec. This offer is limited to one order per household. Not valid for current subscribers to Love Inspired books. All orders subject to credit approval. Credit or debit balances in a customer's account(s) may be offset by any other outstanding balance owed by or to the customer. Please allow 4 to 6 weeks for delivery. Offer available while quantities last.

Your Privacy—The Harlequin® Reader Service is committed to protecting your privacy. Our Privacy Policy is available online at www.ReaderService.com or upon request from the Harlequin Reader Service.

We make a portion of our mailing list available to reputable third parties that offer products we believe may interest you. If you prefer that we not exchange your name with third parties, or if you wish to clarify or modify your communication preferences, please visit us at www.ReaderService.com/consumerschoice or write to us at Harlequin Reader Service Preference Service, P.O. Box 9062, Buffalo, NY 14269. Include your complete name and address.

LI13R

SADDLE UP AND READ 'EM!

This summer, get your fix of Western reads and pick up a cowboy from the INSPIRATIONAL category in July!

THE OUTLAW'S REDEMPTION
by Renee Ryan
from Love Inspired Historical

MONTANA WRANGLER
by Charlotte Carter
from Love Inspired

*Look for these great Western reads AND MORE,
available wherever books are sold or visit*
www.Harlequin.com/Westerns